S0-AJX-826

Don't look behind you!

The shadow of a man appeared seemingly out of nowhere and lunged at her. She pivoted, trying to scramble away. But she wasn't fast enough, and a hard body plowed into her with the force of a Sherman tank.

Strong arms clamped around her like a vise and tackled her to the ground. Spitting dirt, she rolled and lashed out with both feet. Satisfaction flicked in her brain when her assailant grunted. The next thing she knew he was on top of her. With her arms bound, she could not defend herself.

"Get off me!" she shouted.

She caught a glimpse of dark eyes. She felt the tremendous force of his strength, and her only thought was that these were the last moments of her life.

"If you want to live, you'll be quiet."

LINDA CASTILLO

OPERATION: MIDNIGHT GUARDIAN

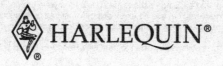

HARLEQUIN®

TORONTO • NEW YORK • LONDON
AMSTERDAM • PARIS • SYDNEY • HAMBURG
STOCKHOLM • ATHENS • TOKYO • MILAN • MADRID
PRAGUE • WARSAW • BUDAPEST • AUCKLAND

ISBN 0-373-88694-2

OPERATION: MIDNIGHT GUARDIAN

ABOUT THE AUTHOR

Linda Castillo knew at a very young age that she wanted to be a writer—and penned her first novel at the age of thirteen. She is the winner of numerous writing awards, including the Holt Medallion, the Golden Heart, the Daphne du Maurier and received a nomination for the prestigious RITA® Award.

Linda loves writing edgy romantic suspense novels that push the envelope and take her readers on a roller-coaster ride of breathtaking romance and thrilling suspense. She resides in Texas with her husband, four lovable dogs and an Appaloosa named George. For a complete list of her books, check out her Web site at www.lindacastillo.com. Contact her at books@lindacastillo.com. Or write to her at P.O. Box 670501, Dallas, Texas 75367-0501.

Books by Linda Castillo

HARLEQUIN INTRIGUE
871—OPERATION: MIDNIGHT TANGO
890—OPERATION: MIDNIGHT ESCAPE
920—OPERATION: MIDNIGHT GUARDIAN

CAST OF CHARACTERS

Sean Cutter—It is the mission of a lifetime: apprehend escaped prisoner Mattie Logan before a terrorist cell can retrieve the secrets locked inside her head. Will his heart survive an encounter with the angel-faced beauty?

Mattie Logan—A brilliant former Department of Defense scientist, did she sell her soul for the likes of money? Or was she framed by someone she trusted?

Daniel Savage—Is he an innocent Department of Defense coworker willing to risk his career to help Mattie? Or is he the man responsible for framing her?

The Jaguar—A cruel terrorist with a personal vendetta against Sean Cutter. He will do anything to obtain the secret locked inside Mattie Logan's head. Will he get to her before Cutter?

Mike Madrid—He is the man Cutter calls when the going gets rough and lives are on the line. But is he willing to go the distance to save the life of an alleged traitor?

Martin Wolfe—He's at the very top of the CIA food chain. He wants the Jaguar caught at any cost. But does he deem Mattie Logan expendable?

Prologue

The prison van swayed rhythmically as it barreled into the night, but Mattie Logan didn't sleep. The judge's final word rang like a death knell in her ears.

Guilty.

The verdict had been handed down eight hours earlier in the federal courthouse in Billings, Montana. She couldn't believe she would be spending the rest of her life in prison. How in the name of God had this happened?

She'd asked herself that question a thousand times in the past four months. Four agonizing months spent in a prison cell the size of a bathroom. A cell where she'd come very close to losing her mind. The only thing that had kept her going was the promise of justice. The hope that truth would prevail. Eight hours ago that hope had been ripped from her desperate grasp, and she was left with nothing but a keen sense of impending doom.

Mattie Logan, you are hereby sentenced to life in prison.

When she shifted on the bench seat, the shackles on her ankles and wrists rattled. The U.S. Marshal sitting across from her glanced at her over the top of his magazine but didn't offer to loosen the cuffs. Because of the nature of her alleged crime, she'd been deemed a high security risk. The term was laughable—or terrifying, depending on your point of view. Nonetheless, three U.S. Marshals had been assigned to transport her from Billings to a federal prison facility at an undisclosed location in Washington State.

Mattie gazed out the small window at

the stark winter-dead trees silhouetted against a jagged horizon. They were traveling on a desolate stretch of highway somewhere in the mountains and heading west. The bleak scene reminded her of her life—cold and desolate—and at that moment she'd never felt more alone.

She leaned against the seat back and tried not to think. But her scientist's mind was always at work. It was one of the reasons she'd been hired to work on the top-secret EDNA project at the Department of Defense.

If only she'd known....

A loud bang disrupted the silence. The van swerved violently, tossing her against the wall. Mattie looked over to see the young marshal rise, his expression alarmed, his hand going to his sidearm. Had a tire blown?

Then a second bang sounded. The van veered left, the force throwing Mattie to the floor. A few feet away the young marshal clutched the balance bar as he stumbled toward the cab, his eyes trained on the driver.

"Sam, what happened?" he shouted. *"Sam!"*

The driver didn't answer. Through the windshield Mattie saw the headlights play wildly over brush and sapling trees. Fear cut through her when she realized the van was careening into a ravine.

A violent bump sent her two feet into the air. The marshal stumbled and fell but didn't drop his radio. "Bravo Victor Two Niner. We got a code—"

His voice was cut off as the van pitched. Mattie caught a glimpse of the driver slumped over the wheel. Out the window, she saw sparks and debris spew high into the air. Another lurch tossed her to the opposite side of the van and sent the marshal sliding across the floor. The female marshal was shouting as she grappled for her radio.

The lights blinked out, plunging them into darkness. The floor tilted, and Mattie began to tumble. She tried to raise her arms to protect herself, but the cuffs and shackles hindered her. A sound that was part scream, part moan tore from her throat when her head snapped back, shattering glass.

Then suddenly the van was still. In total darkness Mattie lay on her back. Somewhere nearby steam hissed. The side door was now above her and stood open. Cold air poured in, embracing her with icy fingers. Beyond, a sliver of moon illuminated fast-moving storm clouds.

The female marshal called out. "Is everyone all right?"

"I think my leg's broke," came a weak voice.

"What the hell happened?" came a third.

"Logan? You okay?"

Mattie did a quick physical inventory. Her head hurt. Raising her hand, she touched her temple, felt the wetness of blood. "I'm cut."

"Stay put." One male marshal groaned as he rose.

"What about Sam?" the female marshal asked, referring to the driver.

Mattie looked toward the cab. By the light of the moon she could see that the driver was slumped across the seat at an odd angle.

"I'll check." One of the male marshals went to the driver.

"We've got an engine fire," came another voice.

"Let's get everyone out of the van."

Mattie shoved herself to a sitting position and looked around. Through the cab window she saw the yellow flicker of flames coming from the engine. Somewhere in the van, the injured marshal groaned in pain.

The other male marshal came up beside her and squatted. "I'm going to take the shackles off your ankles so you can climb out."

Still numb with shock, Mattie nodded. "Okay."

Quickly he removed the shackles and tossed them aside. Leaving the handcuffs in place, he took her arm firmly and guided her toward the open door where the female agent was waiting. "Get the prisoner to a safe place and keep an eye on her. Get on the radio and get an ambulance and the local sheriff's office here ASAP. I'm going to get Sam out in case the van blows."

"Roger that." The female marshal heaved herself through the open door, then leaned down and offered her hand to Mattie. "Come on."

Mattie braced her feet on the seat back and let the woman pull her from the van. Cold night air engulfed her as she emerged. She smelled gasoline and smoke. Felt heat from the engine fire. The female marshal pointed to a fallen log several yards away. "Sit down and don't move. You got that?"

On shaking legs Mattie stumbled over to the log and sat down hard. She didn't know if it was from cold or shock, but she couldn't seem to stop shaking. The van had ended up on its side thirty-five feet down a treacherously steep ravine. The interior lights were out, but a single dim headlight shot a beam through the darkness, exposing a cliff that surely would have killed all onboard had the van gone over.

The female marshal tugged her radio from her belt. "This is Bravo Victor Two Niner—"

A soft *thwack!* sounded. Startled by the sound, Mattie looked up in time to see the female marshal collapse. Concerned, she rushed to the fallen woman and knelt.

"Are you all right?" she asked.

At first she though the marshal had succumbed to some injury sustained in the crash. Panic hit when she found herself looking at a hole the size of a dime in the woman's forehead.

"Oh my God." Mattie staggered back. She looked around, spotted the two male marshals climbing out of the van. "I think she's been shot!" she cried.

The two men looked at her. "What are you talking about?"

Thwack! Thwack! Thwack!

Both marshals jerked as if an overzealous puppeteer had yanked invisible strings. Something dark and shiny bloomed on one of the men's jacket. They collapsed and lay still.

Mattie stared at the fallen men in disbelief. Someone was shooting at them, but she couldn't fathom who or why. What was going on?

A light slashed through the darkness at the top of the ravine. Relief swept through her when four men emerged from a black SUV. She was about to call out to them when it struck her that they were speaking in a language she wasn't familiar with. Who were they? How had they arrived on the scene so quickly?

Instinct sent her slinking behind the fallen log. From her hiding place, she watched as they started toward the wreckage and the downed U.S. Marshals. Were these men rescuers? Or were they the shooters?

One of the men stopped at the nearest fallen marshal. "Where is your prisoner?" he asked in a heavily accented voice.

The marshal groaned. "Help us…"

"Where is your prisoner?" the man repeated.

"Got…away," the marshal groaned.

The man drew back a booted foot and kicked the marshal. *"Where is she!"*

The marshal ground out a curse. "Screw… you."

Hissing a word Mattie didn't understand, the man pulled a gun from his belt. "Stupid American," he said and shot the marshal at point-blank range.

Horrified, Mattie scrambled back, put her hand over her mouth to keep herself from screaming. She'd never seen anything so brutal in her life. Who were these men? Why had they shot that marshal in cold blood? And why were they looking for her?

But deep inside, Mattie knew what they wanted. The knowledge terrified her almost as much as the brutality she'd just witnessed.

The killer stepped back, his eyes skimming the area, a predator hungry for a kill. Mattie instinctively sank closer to the ground.

"Check the van!" he shouted to the other three men. "Find the scientist. I want her alive!"

Knowing she would be discovered within minutes if she didn't get out of there, she frantically looked around. But there was no place to run. No place to hide. Oh dear God what now?

The ravine offered her only route of escape. It was steep and rocky and as black as an abyss, but if she wanted to live she was going to have to risk it. Silently she slithered on her belly to the edge of the cliff.

"There are tracks here!" came a gruff male voice scant yards behind her.

"Spread out!" came the killer's voice. "I want her found!"

Gripping an exposed root, Mattie slid over the ledge. Her feet dangled. She could hear rocks falling below. Saying a silent prayer, she let go of the root and tumbled into space.

Chapter One

Sean Cutter knew from experience that good news never came in the dead of night. For an instant he considered not answering his cell phone.

"Cutter," he growled.

"It's Martin."

Uneasy surprise rippled through him at the sound of his former superior's voice. Martin Wolfe was CIA and at the very top of the agency food chain. At one time the two men had been friends, but that friendship had ended a year ago when Cutter walked away from a career he'd invested twelve years of his life in. A fact that made this call at two o'clock in the morning all the more ominous.

"Why in the bloody hell are you calling me at this hour?" Cutter snapped. But he'd always known the call would come. He'd known one day they would want him back, that he wouldn't be able to refuse.

"The Jaguar is in the country," Wolfe said.

The name slammed into Cutter like a fist. For several interminable seconds he couldn't speak.

"You there?"

Shaking himself mentally, Cutter sat up, threw his legs over the side of the bed. "Talk to me."

"I got three dead U.S. Marshals and a missing Defense Department scientist. The Jaguar wants the scientist."

Cutter got a bad feeling in the pit of his stomach. "Why?"

"She was the brain behind the EDNA Project."

The situation solidified in a terrible

rush. The EDNA Project was a top-secret weapons program funded by the Department of Defense. Though his knowledge of the weapon itself was limited, he knew DOD had been developing a new generation of weapons. A technology The Jaguar would do anything to obtain. If he got his hands on the scientist, he would possess a weapon the likes of which mankind had never seen.

"Martin, I've been out of the CIA for two year—"

"I need you back, Sean. I don't have to tell you what this son of a bitch is capable of."

Cutter knew exactly what The Jaguar was capable of. He had the scars to prove it. And even after two years, he still had the nightmares…

"If he gets his hands on EDNA, every city in the world will be at risk of being incinerated. We can't let that happen."

Cutter closed his eyes, the gravity of the situation sinking in. "Why me?"

"Because you know The Jaguar better than anyone. You've got the training. The experience."

The killer instinct, Cutter thought darkly and felt a little sick. After what happened on his last mission, he'd sworn never again…

A refusal teetered on his lips, but he didn't voice it. Sean Cutter might have walked away from his career, but he never walked away from duty. Not even when he knew it could probably kill him.

"I want you to find the scientist before The Jaguar does, and bring her in."

It seemed a simple assignment on the surface. But Cutter knew there was more. With Martin Wolfe, there was always more. "What else?"

"I want you to bring The Jaguar in this time, Sean. Homeland Security has given me forty-eight hours to get this done. After that I have to take this public. Bring in local law enforcement and FBI."

"And if The Jaguar gets to her before I do?"

"You have the authority to do whatever it takes to make sure she doesn't talk."

"What are you saying, Martin?"

"I'm saying she's expendable. If the situation boils down to her life or the population of Los Angeles or New York or Houston, I want you to take her out."

Cutter closed his eyes, dread seeping from every pore like fear sweat.

"I'll catch the next flight out."

"I've got a Lear waiting."

"Pretty damn sure of yourself, aren't you?"

"No, but I am sure of you."

If only you knew, Cutter thought, and disconnected.

He sat down hard on the bed, dread roiling in his gut. Putting his face in his hands, he tried not to think about what he'd done.

IN THE PREDAWN DARKNESS, Mattie took the trail at a reckless speed. The cuffs binding her hands hindered, but she didn't slow down. Her labored breaths echoed against the canyon walls. A cold wind swept through the gorge, whipping the trees into a frenzy.

She'd been running for what seemed like hours. She didn't know where she was or where she was going, raw panic driving her forward. All she knew was if she stopped she would die.

She couldn't believe her life had come to this. One short year ago she'd been living comfortably in a Washington, D.C., suburb. She'd driven her little blue Jetta to work every morning. She'd been happy. Challenged by her work. And falling for her attractive coworker, Daniel Savage. Everything had come to a grinding halt the day two grim-faced CIA agents walked into her office and arrested her for treason.

Treason.

Even now the insanity of the charge still stunned her. Overhead a spear of lightning split the sky. Mattie ducked reflexively but she didn't slow her pace. She knew it would take a miracle, but if she could reach a phone, she could call Daniel. He would know what to do. He would help her if she asked, even if it meant risking his own reputation to do it. All she had to do was find a house or passing motorist.

Something rustled in the brush to her right. Biting back a cry, Mattie veered left. *Don't stop!* the little voice inside her head chanted. *Don't look behind you!*

The shadow of a man appeared seemingly out of nowhere and lunged at her. She pivoted, trying to scramble away. But she wasn't fast enough, and a hard body plowed into her with the force of a Sherman tank.

Mattie had expected claws and teeth or maybe an expedient shot to the head. Instead, strong arms clamped around her like a vise and tackled her to the ground. Spitting dirt, she rolled and lashed out with both feet. Satisfaction flicked in her brain when her assailant grunted. The next thing she knew he was on top of her. With her arms bound she could not defend herself.

"Get off me!" she shouted.

She caught a glimpse of dark eyes. She felt the tremendous force of his strength, and her only thought was that these were the last moments of her life.

"If you want to live you'll be quiet."

Mattie barely heard the rough whisper over the wild pounding of her heart. She tried to twist away, but he was heavy and strong, pinning her with ease.

"What do you—"

A hand slapped over her mouth, cutting her words short. "Shh."

Mattie stilled, and for an instant the only sound came from their labored breaths and the tinkle of sleet against dry leaves. Blinking hair from her eyes, she looked up, found herself staring into icy, blue eyes.

"There are four heavily armed men less than two hundred yards away," he said in a low voice. "Make another sound and they'll kill us both. Do you understand?"

For an instant the sense of helplessness and terror nearly overwhelmed her. But Mattie could tell by the look in his eyes that if he wanted her dead, he would have already done it.

She jerked her head. Never taking his eyes from hers, he removed his hand from her mouth and put his finger to his lips. His eyes scanned the surrounding darkness. Reaching out, he grasped the base of a long-dead bush and dragged it over them. The bush was large and full and in the semidarkness would cover them completely.

He turned to her and looked into her eyes, his expression tense. He was lying squarely on top of her with some of his weight on his elbows. "Don't move," he whispered. "I'm not going to hurt you."

His body was rock hard, his muscles

taut. At some point during the struggle her legs had opened, and he was lying between her knees, pressed intimately against her. He was no longer breathing hard, but she was.

"The tracks end here!" A heavily accented voice cut through the night like a blade.

"She's using the stream to hide her tracks." Another voice. Frighteningly near.

"We should have had her by now. We're running out of time."

Mattie listened, praying they wouldn't be discovered when she saw a pair of boots and the butt of a semiautomatic rifle a few yards to her right. He was standing so close she could smell the stench of his sweat. Her breaths grew rapid and shallow.

"We're safe," the man lying on top of her whispered. "Just calm down."

In the last hours she'd seen too much violence to keep a handle on the fear barreling through her. She could feel her entire body vibrating as a fresh wave of

panic engulfed her. She began to hyper-
ventilate. Her face and hands were
tingling. If she didn't get a grip, she was
going to give away their hiding place and
get them both killed.

Dry grass crunched as one of the killers
drew closer. For a terrible instant Mattie
thought he'd heard her panicked breathing. She imagined him raising the rifle
and shooting them the same way he'd
gunned down the three marshals. The
urge to jump to her feet and run was
strong. She could feel her muscles twitch-
ing as the flight instinct kicked in.

"Easy," the man lying on top of her
whispered. "Slow, deep breaths."

But Mattie was beyond hearing, beyond
logic. She tried breathing through her
nose, but she could no more slow her
breathing than a marathon runner who'd
just run ten miles.

Grass and leaves rustled nearby and she
knew one of the men was approaching. *This
is it*, she thought. *I've given away our*

hiding place and now they're going to kill us.

The man on top of her shifted, and suddenly she was aware of the way his body fit against hers. Surprising her, he set his hands on either side of her face. His palms were warm and amazingly gentle as he brushed back the hair from her face. Mattie looked into the startling blue of his eyes. And even though the threat of death was so close she could feel the cold scrape of it against her spine, her only thought was that no man had ever looked at her the way this man did.

"What are you doing?" she asked.

"Saving our lives," he said and lowered his mouth to hers.

CUTTER CONSIDERED HIMSELF a master of improvisation. He possessed an uncanny talent for making the best of a bad situation and the ability to adapt to current conditions. They were traits that made him the best of the best. At the moment, kissing this woman seemed like the most expedient way to keep her from getting both of them killed.

He hadn't expected to get caught up in the softness of her mouth. Sean Cutter didn't get caught up in anything, especially when it came to his job. But that was exactly what happened when his mouth made contact with hers.

She tried to turn her head, but he caught her cheek with his palm and deepened the kiss. She opened her mouth—to protest no doubt—and he seized the opportunity to take the kiss deeper. *Another mistake,* he thought dazedly, but by then he'd stopped counting.

Her mouth was warm and wet against his. Her body was curvy and soft and fit perfectly beneath him. He could feel the warmth of her quickened breaths against his cheek. And despite the fact that they were seconds away from being discovered by four men who would not hesitate to execute them, he found his body responding to hers.

He struggled to control the hot rush of blood to his groin, reminding himself of all the terrible things that could happen next. But her mouth was incredibly soft, her body a promise of all the things he'd denied himself for what felt like a lifetime. And while Cutter was a whiz at improvisation, he hadn't a clue how to stanch good-old-fashioned sexual arousal—no matter how dangerous.

But the kiss was working. Slowly her body relaxed against his, and her breathing slowed. Cutter broke the kiss and for several agonizing minutes neither of them moved while the four killers smoked cigarettes and spoke in a language he was all too familiar with. If the woman could feel his erection against her, she gave no indication. She was probably too terrified to notice. He should be, too, considering they were inches away from getting shot. But Cutter had already faced the worst thing a man could face. He didn't have a death wish, but not much truly scared him anymore.

After what seemed like an eternity, the men moved on. Cutter lay on top of his prisoner for several more minutes, listening to the men's retreat. Once he deemed it safe, he tossed the bush aside and rose.

"What the hell do you think you're doing?" Glaring at him, the woman sat up and with cuffed hands brushed at the leaves and dust on her clothes.

"Saving your life."

A twig was sticking out of her hair. She was still wearing the slacks and jacket she'd worn to court. Both knees of her slacks were torn. The top button of her blouse had popped off at some point and he could see the lacy outline of her bra. Damn.

"You had no right to…to—"

"You were hyperventilating. If I hadn't done something, you would have gotten both of us killed."

Even in the semidarkness, he saw her pale. "Who are you?"

"I'm the man who's going to take you back. For now, that's all you need to know."

"I don't want to go back."

He jabbed a thumb in the direction of where the four men had disappeared. "Maybe you'd rather take your chances with those cutthroats."

"I'm innocent."

Cutter couldn't help it. He laughed. "Yeah, so am I." Bending, he grasped her bicep to help her up.

"I'm not going anywhere with you," she said as she got to her feet.

"Here's a newsflash for you, blondie. You don't have a say in the matter."

Of their own accord, his eyes did a quick sweep down the front of her. Even though her suit was rumpled and torn, he could see that she was slender and willowy and built just the way he liked. Her hands were cuffed, accentuating curves he had no right noticing at a time like this.

He removed the master key from his belt. "Give me your wrists."

She blinked. "You're uncuffing me?"

"We need to move quickly before those bozos realize they fell for the oldest trick in the book." He glanced up at the sky. Storm clouds were billowing to the northwest. The weather had been an issue during his briefing in the Lear jet that had taken him from Chicago to a small airport in Kalispell, Montana. A cold front chock-full of nasty precipitation was barreling down from the Canadian border. Cutter figured they had another hour before the skies opened up. Hopefully, enough time to make it to the rendezvous point where the agency had a chopper waiting.

She offered her wrists. "Who were those men?"

"Old friends of yours, no doubt."

"I don't know what you're talking about."

But a tremor went through her as he removed the cuffs. A shiver that didn't have anything to do with the cold and told him she knew exactly what he was talking about. "Save it for your appeal," he snapped, and shoved the cuffs into a compartment in his belt.

She turned to him, her eyes wide and beseeching. "I don't know those men. And I didn't do anything wrong."

Another laugh squeezed from his throat, only this time it was bitter. "You sold out your country. As far as I'm concerned that puts you on the same level as those animals searching for you."

As a man who had dedicated most of his adult life to protecting the country he loved, the thought of someone selling out for the likes of money disgusted him beyond words.

The problem was Mattie Logan didn't look like a traitor. Blue eyed and blond haired, she looked wholesome and kind. But Cutter knew all too well that looks could be deceiving. Mattie Logan might look like the girl next door, but a traitor lay beneath the innocent facade. Remembering the way his body had reacted to her just a few short minutes earlier, he silently reprimanded himself for his weakness and vowed not to let himself be taken in again.

"I didn't do any of what they accused me of," she said.

"I don't care." And he didn't. Not one iota. All he cared about at the moment was getting her to the chopper-pick-up location an hour to the south. "Let's go."

"Please," she said. "You have to believe me."

"I don't have to do squat."

"I would never compromise EDNA. That project was the greatest achievement of my career. I safeguarded it with my life."

Cutter didn't know the details of her case. All he knew was that she'd been found guilty of treason in a court of law. He trusted the justice system. It was his job to take her back. Black and white, just the way he liked it. Then he could move on to the most challenging phase of his mission: finding The Jaguar and bringing him to justice.

"Someone framed me," she said. "It's the only explanation."

"If you don't start walking, I'm going to put the cuffs back on and drag you down that trail."

Rubbing her wrists where bruises had formed, she turned and started walking. "Don't you care about justice?"

"Justice for whom?" Cutter usually didn't indulge his prisoners in conversation, but her denials were beginning to annoy him. "The millions of people you endangered by selling EDNA? Did you happen to think about that?"

She started to turn and face him, but Cutter reached out and stopped her by grasping her arm. He wanted to believe he'd kept her moving because he was in a hurry to get to the rendezvous point. But deep inside he acknowledged that he did not want to look into those pretty blue eyes and know what she was. Beauty and evil just did not go together.

"I meant what I said about dragging you," he warned.

"Please. I can't go to prison for a crime I didn't commit. You have to listen to me."

"Do you have any idea how many times I've heard that?"

"It's the truth! I'm innocent!"

"Take it up with the courts, sweetheart. Right now you have a date with a chopper, and come hell or high water I'm going to make sure you don't miss it."

Chapter Two

Dawn broke with a monochromatic sky and the tinkle of sleet against the ground. In the distance thunder rumbled menacingly. The hopelessness of her situation pressed down on Mattie like a lead weight as she made her way down the rugged trail. The last thing she wanted to do was get on that chopper and be transported to prison, but she knew if she tried to make a run for it, the man who'd apprehended her would stop her.

Mattie Logan, you are hereby sentenced to life in prison.

The words echoed until she thought she would scream with the injustice of them.

But what could she do? Run? Convince this hard-nosed man she was innocent? Neither option seemed realistic.

"This is Delta Ringo One to Eagle. Do you read?"

Her captor's voice drew her from her reverie. Mattie turned to see him speak into his radio.

"That's affirm, Delta." A voice crackled on the other end.

"I've got the package."

"Roger that."

"What's your twenty on the rendez-vous?"

"Coordinates two five three point one. What's your ETA?"

The man punched numbers into a small device. "Ten minutes."

It was the first time she'd had the chance to study him. He was lean and tall with an expression that told her he was serious about what he did. Wearing faded jeans, high-end hiking boots and a flannel shirt over a turtleneck, he didn't look like any cop she'd ever seen. There was something dangerous about him that had nothing to do with some badge or even the semiautomatic pistol strapped to his hip. Something unpredictable that warned her not to cross him. But Mattie knew if she wanted to clear her name, crossing him was a calculated risk she was going to have to take.

"Be advised we have heavy weather coming in," the voice barked from the radio.

"Time frame?"

"Front's here, Delta. Get your butt in gear."

"Roger that." Frowning, he shoved the radio and hand-held device into his backpack and shot her with a dark look. "You heard the man, blondie. Let's pick up the pace."

For a crazy instant she considered making a run for it. Now that her hands were free, she would be able to run unencumbered. With a storm approaching, maybe her captor would be forced to return to the chopper without her. She envisioned herself barreling down the ravine to her left. If she could reach the stream…

"Don't even think about it."

Mattie glanced at him. Fifteen feet separated them. Not much of a head start, but suddenly she knew this moment would probably be her last chance for escape.

"I can't go back," she said.

"Don't do anything stupid."

"I know you don't believe me, but I'm innocent. I swear on my life. All I need is the chance to prove it."

"You're not going to get the chance out here in the middle of nowhere."

It's now or never…

Mattie broke into a sprint toward the stream at the base of the ravine. She crashed through the brush, veered left to avoid a stand of sapling pines. She could hear his occasional curse behind her as his heavy boots pounded the ground. She ran as she had never run before, hurdling over fallen logs and rocks the size of basketballs. Her only thought was that if he caught her, her life would be over.

The next thing she knew, his strong arms were wrapped around her from behind. She screamed as he dragged her down. She fell hard on her stomach, twisted and lashed out with both feet.

He grunted when her heel caught his chin. She saw his head snap back, caught a glimpse of his angry eyes and a slash of blood where her heel had cut him.

"Stop resisting!" he growled.

But Mattie was fighting for her life. She'd been locked up for four months like an animal for an unspeakable crime she hadn't committed. Her only hope of salvaging her life was escape. She'd decided a long time ago that she would rather die than spend the rest of her life in a cage.

But he was incredibly strong. An animal sound tore from her throat as he pinned her to the ground. He was sitting on her abdomen, his hands manacling her wrists above her head.

"Pull yourself together," he snapped.

"I'm not going with you," Mattie panted.

"You don't have a say in the matter."

Helplessness and impotent rage burned through her. To her horror, tears welled. Humiliated, Mattie tried to turn away, but he held her flat.

"You've left me no choice but to cuff you," he said.

Mattie hated the cuffs; they made her feel like a criminal. He snapped the nylon restraints into place—in front—which made them marginally more comfortable.

He rose and helped her to her feet. "If you have a beef with the verdict, you've got to handle it through the courts. Not out here. There's a dangerous storm on the way and four killers who will stop at nothing to get whatever secrets you have locked inside your head. Do you understand?"

"What I understand," she said in a

trembling voice, "is that neither justice nor my life means anything to you."

He studied her as if she were a puzzle missing a vital piece, then he motioned toward the trail. "When we get to the chopper I'll clean up that cut on your temple."

The cut was so inconsequential when her life was destroyed that Mattie choked back a hysterical laugh. "Like that's going to make everything all better."

"Lady, I'm just doing my job the best way I know how. If you're as smart as your file claims you are, you'll make it easier on both of us and cooperate."

"I will play no role in the ruination of my life."

"You should have thought about that before you got involved with those thugs." He jammed his thumb in the direction from which they'd come. "If those bastards get their hands on you, you will find out the true meaning of brutality."

"I'd rather die than spend the rest of my life in prison."

"Keep it up and you'll get your wish." He looked at his watch. "Now let's move out."

He set a grueling pace as they trekked toward the pick-up location. Mattie felt as if she were walking toward the firing squad. She couldn't believe she'd blown her only chance of escape.

Within minutes, the *Whop! Whop! Whop!* of the chopper's rotor blades rent the air. Through the trees she spotted the large craft perched on a rocky ridge in a clearing. The fuselage was yellow with black lettering.

They were twenty yards away when a man in khaki pants and a parka opened the chopper's hatch and stepped out. "About damn time," he said, his eyes going from her captor to her and lingering.

Mattie looked away, wondering if this would be the last time she saw trees, the last time she breathed in mountain air and freedom.

"She give you any problems?" the man asked.

Her captor gave her a measuring look. "None I couldn't handle."

"Get her in the chopper. Pilot's RTG. Let's see if we can beat this cold front."

Her captor took her arm and led her toward the chopper. She was about to step inside when a gunshot stopped her dead in her tracks. She spun to see the man in khakis crumple to the ground.

"Holy hell! Rusty!"

Her captor went for his weapon, but he wasn't fast enough. A third man in a flight suit emerged from the chopper leveling a deadly looking weapon at her captor's chest.

"Drop the gun, Cutter, or I swear you'll join him."

THERE WAS NOTHING Sean Cutter hated more than a traitor. That deep-seated hatred boiled inside him as he stared at the CIA chopper pilot he'd known and trusted for the better part of his professional life.

"What the hell are you doing, Meeks?"

"What do you think?" Grimacing, the pilot jumped from the chopper to the ground, his eyes flashing from Cutter to Mattie.

"I think you're selling your soul," Cutter said.

"What can I say? They pay better than Uncle Sam." Meeks crossed to Mattie and licked his lips. She cringed when he ran a fingertip from her chin, down her neck to her shoulder. "I don't know why The Jaguar wants you so badly, but he made me an offer I couldn't refuse."

"How much?" Cutter asked.

"A million and change."

"Generous."

"I thought so. A hell of a lot more than a CIA pilot will ever see in his lifetime."

"Too bad you won't live to spend it."

Cutter edged closer, but Meeks smiled and set his finger against the trigger. "Don't get any closer, Sean. You know I'll put a bullet in you."

Cutter glanced down at the man lying on the ground in a widening pool of blood. "Evidently you don't have any qualms about taking out one of your own."

"Not one of my own. I'm a free agent now."

"You're a coward and a traitor."

The pilot smiled. "But very rich."

"So tell me, Meeks. How does this work? You kill two federal agents and deliver a DOD scientist to a terrorist group? You think they're really going to pay you?"

"I've already got half of it."

"And you think the CIA is going to walk away and let you live happily ever after?"

"I'll be able to afford to get lost anywhere in the world."

"There's no place remote enough on this earth that will keep the CIA from finding you."

"Unless they think I'm dead." His eyes flicked to the pistol at Sean's hip. "Give me your weapon, GPS unit and radio."

When Cutter hesitated, the other man pulled back the slide on the weapon. "Do it or I'll take out your kneecaps first."

Hoping to buy time, Cutter pulled the radio and GPS unit from his belt and tossed both to the ground.

Meeks stepped forward and crushed the radio beneath his boot. "The gun, too, Cutter. Stop wasting my time."

Relinquishing his weapon was the one thing Cutter would not do. He knew Meeks was going to kill him, then deliver this scientist to a dangerous terrorist cell. If he wanted to prevent both of those things from happening he was going to have to make a move.

Putting his hand on his weapon, he stepped closer. "You son of a bitch."

Cutter's nerves jigged when the other man shifted the gun to his chest. "Nice and slow. The gun. Now."

Cutter went for his weapon, brought up the muzzle. But he wasn't fast enough. The other man fired. The bullet struck him in the chest like a baseball bat slamming in a homerun. The breath left his lungs in a sound that was half roar, half curse. He reeled backward, lost his footing. The next thing he knew his back hit the ground. Pain radiated through his chest. He couldn't move. Couldn't breathe. Dizziness descended like a fast-acting narcotic.

Through the haze of pain Cutter was aware of the pilot pointing the weapon at the woman. "Get in the chopper, bitch."

Cutter felt himself fading in and out of consciousness. But there was no way he could let Meeks fly out with Mattie Logan in tow. She was a walking time bomb. If The Jaguar got his hands on her, the world would pay a terrible price.

He tried to sit up, but searing pain sent him back down. He tried to draw a breath, succeeded only in making an undignified sound. Damn. He hadn't wanted things to end this way...

He was wondering how the situation could get any worse when four men wielding semiautomatic rifles stormed the clearing.

SHE WAS GOING TO DIE. If not by the hand of the pilot, then certainly by one of the gunmen. Two minutes ago her biggest concern had been clearing her name. Now, at the mercy of five brutal killers, she figured she'd be lucky to walk away in one piece.

Mattie couldn't take her eyes off the man called Cutter as he lay on the ground a few feet away. A crimson stain the size of a saucer bloomed on his shirt. She hadn't wanted to go back with him, but she certainly hadn't wanted to see him shot down like an animal.

She stood frozen, her heart pounding wildly as the four men verged on the pilot. The leader of the group was a thin man of average height. His coal-black hair was swept back from a high forehead. Eyes the color of midnight swept from the man on the ground, to Mattie.

"I see you are a man of your word," he said to the pilot.

"Signed, sealed and delivered," the pilot replied.

The man's black eyes swept down the front of her. "You are not what I expected."

"I don't know anything," she blurted.

Sick amusement danced in his eyes. "What you know remains to be seen, doesn't it?"

She jolted when he raised his hand and brushed her jaw with his knuckle. "It makes no difference to me if you are a woman or a man. One way or another, you *will* tell me everything you know about the final phase of EDNA or I will hurt you in ways you could never imagine."

She believed him. And suddenly she was very sorry the man who'd come to take her back was lying on the ground, dying.

The terrorist motioned toward the fallen agent. "What happened?"

"He made a move." The pilot shrugged. "I had to take him out."

"I told you I wanted him alive. Sean Cutter and I have unfinished business."

"He didn't give me a choice."

The other man's expression darkened, but he said nothing.

The pilot glanced toward dark clouds roiling on the horizon. "Look, there's a storm moving in. Pay me that last half of the money and I'll drop you and your associates wherever you need to go. But we've got to move now or else risk getting stranded on this godforsaken mountain."

For the first time Mattie realized that in

the last few minutes the wind had picked up. Snow mixed with sleet was swirling around the treetops. A thin layer already covered the ground.

She knew these men were going to kill her. The ringleader had all but promised to torture her for information about EDNA. Once they got what they wanted from her, she would be expendable. A chill that had nothing to do with the cold snaked through her at the thought of the horrors she faced in the coming hours....

"Get in the chopper," the ringleader said to his men.

"I can take you as far as Canada," the pilot said as they started toward the hatch.

"Excellent," the terrorist said. "Let's go."

As the pilot stepped into the craft, the terrorist raised his handgun and fired a single shot. Blood spattered the yellow fuselage. The pilot pitched forward and landed on the ground with a thud.

"That's for killing Sean Cutter," the terrorist muttered.

Horror and disbelief pummeled her like fists. Another man dead. All because these men wanted the plans for the final phase of EDNA....

She wondered how long she would hold up under torture. She wondered how terrible it would be. And in that instant she decided there was no way she could let them take her alive.

"Fire!"

Mattie glanced toward the chopper to see black smoke billowing from its fuselage. Surprised shouts erupted all around her. The men scrambled from the craft. "Grab the extinguisher!" one of them shouted.

"Watch the woman!"

"The fire is coming from the engine! Quickly, put it out!"

Run!

The flight instinct kicked in with a vengeance. Refusing to think of repercussions, she spun away from the chopper and literally ran for her life.

She darted across the clearing to the forest, her feet barely seeming to touch the ground. She scrambled over the trunk of a fallen tree, through brush that tore at her slacks. She knew they would catch her; there was no way she could elude four men with guns. But terror and adrenaline were driving her, not logic.

Shouts erupted as she fled. She heard her pursuers behind her, following her, breaking through brush. Praying for a miracle, she glanced over her shoulder toward the place where the man called Cutter had fallen.

But he was gone.

Chapter Three

Cutter was no stranger to pain. While the Kevlar vest had saved his life, it hadn't prevented the bullet from doing a number on his ribs. The vial of fake blood had helped fool them into believing he was mortally wounded, giving him the chance to start the engine fire as a diversion. But with no weapon, no radio, and four well-armed killers to deal with, staying alive would surely prove to be a tad more difficult.

But it was Mattie Logan who was foremost in his mind as he hurried down the deer trail in search of her. He could hear the men shouting in the distance and knew it would be only a matter of time before they caught up with her. Within minutes of capturing her they would load her onto the chopper and cross the border into Canada. He had no intention of letting that happen.

He turned right at a jut of rock and poured on the speed. Agony tore through his chest with every breath, but he didn't slow down. He didn't let himself think about the pain or the odds he faced. He had to find Logan before the terrorists did....

Operating on little more than animal instinct, he ran toward the tall, dense piñon pines. Logan had fled southwest. If he held his direction, he would intercept her. Hopefully before the others did. But Cutter knew finding her wasn't the toughest challenge he faced. The hard part was going to be getting out of there without getting shot....

The sound of footsteps sent him diving for cover in a blanket of juniper. Peering through the foliage, he caught a glimpse of blond hair and pale skin. He heard the hiss of panicked breaths rushing through clenched teeth.

Logan.

He caught her arm as she passed. Carried by the momentum of her sprint, she stumbled and nearly fell, but Cutter caught her. He slapped a hand over her mouth, catching the scream that would have revealed their position. He felt an impression of soft skin and small bones within his grasp. The hint of lemon and rosemary in silky hair as she swung around. But all of those things were punctuated by panic and terror. A dangerous state if he didn't gain control of the situation pronto.

No time to take her to the ground and subdue her. No time for an explanation. For an instant, she fought back like an animal snared in the deadly teeth of a steel trap. He made eye contact and gave her a hard shake. "If you want to live, come with me," he said in a low voice.

She went still and blinked at him as if waking from a bad dream. "I…I thought you were d-dead."

"So did they, evidently." He looked over his shoulder. "Let's go."

"How do I know I can trust you?"

"You don't," he said and hauled her into a dead run.

A DEAD MAN had saved her life.

It was the only thought Mattie's brain could manage. She didn't know how, but somehow Cutter had survived a gunshot to the chest. Though at the moment, running from men bent on killing them, she didn't necessarily care.

Snow and sleet blinded her as she ran. It took every ounce of physical ability she possessed to keep up with Cutter and maintain her footing. One tiny miscalculation and she would fall—a mistake that would surely prove deadly.

It felt as if they had been running forever. Every muscle in her body ached with exhaustion. Mattie didn't know how she kept going. The primal will to live.

"Whoa. Easy."

She felt a hard tug on her hand. Cutter was pulling her back, slowing her down.

"Can't…stop," she panted.

"It's okay."

"They'll kill us."

"I'm not going to let them kill anyone."

Mattie looked over her shoulder, but the trail they'd just traveled was deserted. She listened for footsteps, but the only sound came from their labored breathing and the soft thud of sleet against the ground.

Giving her a look that told her he was too damn beat to give chase if she decided to take off, Cutter released her, then bent at the hip to gulp air. "We need to rest, catch our breath."

Mattie thought about running, but her legs had evidently decided they'd had enough exertion for one day. When she started to walk away, her knees buckled.

She fell forward onto her hands and knees, and for a moment she could do nothing but breathe.

"Take a moment to catch your breath. Then we've got to keep moving."

Mattie raised her head and glared at him. "It's going to take a lot longer than a moment for me to catch my breath."

They'd stopped in a small clearing. The boughs of the piñon pines were covered with snow. Mattie wondered if they'd gained elevation. If that was why it seemed colder, the air thinner and more difficult to breathe.

"Come on." Cutter crossed to her and extended his hand. "Time to go."

Mattie considered refusing his hand. But she wasn't sure she could rise on her own, so she reached for him. "Back at the chopper, how did you manage the fire?"

"I didn't." He pulled her to her feet. "What you saw was a smoke grenade. A diversion."

No, she thought. *He was no ordinary*

cop. But if he wasn't a cop what agency was he with? CIA? Homeland Security? She wondered why he had been sent to take her back. Why not local law enforcement? Why not the FBI or the U.S. Marshals Service.

"Who are you?" she asked.

"I'm the man who's going to keep you alive." His icy blue eyes burned into hers. "Right now, that's all you need to know."

THE SON OF A BITCH had beaten him at his own game once again.

The Jaguar paced the snow-covered ground with the sleek elegance of his namesake. Dark anticipation and a keen sense of unfinished business had him feeling restless and edgy. Not only was Sean Cutter alive, but he was psychologically and physically sound and working for the CIA again. That more than anything surprised The Jaguar. By all rights, the man should be dead. At the very least he should be locked in a padded cell.

He and the federal agent went way back, but their relationship was far from amicable. Cutter was the only man The Jaguar had not been able to break. Even under torture, the agent had maintained his silence. He'd defied a black art form The Jaguar had made his business and built a reputation upon. The sense of failure had nagged at him for two years. This time, he would make certain Sean Cutter talked, then was tortured and killed.

Bracing himself against the cold north wind, The Jaguar lit a cigarette and walked to the chopper, where two of his men were working on the engine.

"What is the status?" he asked.

"Operable."

"Excellent."

"The smoke was evidently from a smoke grenade and did little damage to the engine."

A diversion, he thought. *How very like Sean Cutter…* Hatred churned inside him.

He looked up at the swirling snow, felt the dark anticipation stir. "Is the chopper equipped with infrared?"

The other man smiled. "The American government spares no expense when it comes to hunting down those who would question their absolute power."

The Jaguar nodded. "I want the scientist and Sean Cutter. I want them alive. And I want them now."

"The weather could be a problem."

He turned his gaze on the other man. "The last man who questioned my wishes lasted for fourteen hours in my torture chamber. When I tired of his screams I shot him. Perhaps you want to test your endurance?"

The other man looked away, his Adam's apple bobbing twice in quick succession. "I am merely looking out for your safety."

"That would best be done once we're airborne."

"I understand."

The Jaguar scanned the rugged countryside, feeling an uncomfortable urgency to finish what should already have been done. "They couldn't have gotten far."

"Not on foot and in this weather. They have no gear. No weapon or radio."

The Jaguar said nothing. But he knew the other man underestimated Sean Cutter. He himself had underestimated the federal agent two years ago. He would not make the same mistake twice.

CUTTER HAD NO PROBLEM with risking his life for the safety and security of the American people. What he didn't like was the idea of risking his life for the likes of a traitor like Mattie Logan. He had zero tolerance for anyone low enough to betray their country.

She might look like an angel with her wide eyes and porcelain skin; she might even be one of the most stunning women he'd ever laid eyes on. But physical beauty made no difference to Cutter when it came to treachery.

He stared at her, keenly aware of her proximity, that she smelled good, that her complexion was as pale and flawless as a child's. But there was nothing even remotely childlike about the rest of her. Her eyes were deep and blue and filled with a woman's secrets. Within their depths he saw the remnants of terror and a jumble of emotions held on a taut rein. Her blond hair was pulled into a ponytail, but several strands had fallen free to frame her face. Strands his fingers itched to brush aside.

She possessed the kind of beauty that blinded a man. The kind of sexual appeal that made even a smart man do stupid things. All for the sound of her laughter or the promise of a touch. An element that made her every bit as dangerous as the terrorists aiming to kill them.

Ignoring the uncomfortable tug of something he didn't want to identify, Cutter turned away. "Let's move. Chances are they're going to use the chopper to search for us."

"But won't the storm ground them?"

"It would if we were dealing with a sane person." He shot her a sober look. "In case you're not reading between the lines here, we're not."

"But they don't have a pilot. They shot him."

Impatient with her questions, he took her hand and pulled her into a jog. "The Jaguar wouldn't have shot him if he didn't have a backup pilot."

"The Jaguar?"

He hadn't meant to say the name aloud. Just hearing it sent a chill up his spine. Even after two years he could recall what it had been like to be helpless and hurting and look into the other man's eyes and see pure evil.

"Stop talking and start moving," he snapped. "Faster."

She complied, but Cutter knew there was little chance of them outdistancing

The Jaguar's men. The terrorist surrounded himself with the most brutal men in the world. Men who would risk it all to advance whatever twisted beliefs had transformed them into terrorists.

Cutter had been in worse situations and still come out alive. But with a storm moving in and killers hot on their trail, survival seemed a long shot at best.

"Where are we going?"

He glanced over at his prisoner. She had snow in her hair. It clung to her thick eyelashes. Her cheeks were pink with cold, her eyes bright with fear. He wished she wasn't so damn good to look at. The last thing he needed was a distraction….

"Right now we're just trying to put some distance between us and those bastards with guns," he said.

She was starting to breathe hard again. The way a woman did when she was in the throes of lovemaking. The image of her with her head thrown back, her body welcoming his, flashed unbidden in his mind's eye. He imagined his hands on her body, her breaths coming short and fast as he worked her toward release….

Shoving the image aside, he picked up the pace. "Faster," he said.

She struggled to keep up. "You never told me what agency you're working for."

"No, I didn't."

"I like to know who I'm dealing with."

"All you need to know is that I'm the man who's going to save your life."

"The way I see it, you're the man who's going to make sure I spend the rest of my life in prison for a crime I didn't commit."

"Save it for the judge, blondie."

"The judge has already made his decision. A decision based on lies and planted evidence."

"You got caught," he snapped. "Deal with it, because you're not going to get any sympathy from me. Got it?"

"What I got is railroaded. I can prove it, but not from inside a prison cell."

"There are young men and women

risking their lives every day to keep this country safe," he snarled. "I don't have any compassion for turncoats, so cut it out."

For several minutes the only sound came from the pounding of their feet against the earth.

"You want to know what's really frightening about all of this?" she asked.

"You have no idea what's really frightening," he said bitterly.

"The real culprit is still out there. They probably have access to the EDNA project. They're probably trying to get their hands on the final-phase plans. And they're probably still planning on selling the information when they do."

Cutter stared hard at her, looking for the lie he knew was there. But the woman staring back at him had one of the most guileless faces he'd ever seen. He was not gullible when it came to female charms. Not by a long shot. But he could feel the draw to her. A draw that was part sexual, part…something else. Like a full moon pulling at a restless sea and causing a dangerously high tide.

Cutter was too smart to act on any of the crazy thoughts running through his head. He knew all too well what could happen when you mixed sex with an assignment. The last time he'd given in to temptation someone had ended up dead. He'd nearly been killed himself and had spent a good part of the next year wishing he hadn't survived.

"Unless you want to end up dead," he said, "you've got to keep moving."

"Maybe that's a better alternative to spending the rest of my life—"

His temper snapped. Stopping abruptly, he swung around to face her. Roughly he yanked her toward him so that her face was only inches from his. Close enough for him to smell the rosemary and lemon of her hair. He steeled himself against the sweet warmth of her breath against his face.

"If you think death is a better alternative than life," he said, "then you haven't seen it up close and personal. Believe me, there's nothing dignified or honorable about it. It's the ugliest thing you'll ever see in your life. So don't make stupid statements like that."

She blinked as if his words had stunned her.

He hadn't meant to lose his temper. Pulling himself back from a place he didn't want to go, Cutter looked around, blew out a curse at the sight of the heavily falling snow. "The good news is that the snow will cover our tracks," he grumbled.

"The way you said that makes me think there's some bad news on the way."

"Yeah, it's called a blizzard."

"At least fate is being consistent."

Not wanting to think about just how bad their luck had been so far, he took her down a small hill and through a forest of sapling aspen and piñon pine that opened to a clearing. A secondary trail ran north and into the higher elevations; to the south was a vertical drop of three hundred feet to the valley floor.

"Which way?" she asked.

"Definitely not down." He stopped a few yards from the edge of the cliff.

She motioned toward a narrow trail that disappeared into a densely wooded area. "Looks like that trail hasn't been used for a while."

"Deer or elk trail probably."

"Where does it go?"

He shrugged. "Into the higher elevations."

"Are there any houses or ranger stations?"

"There used to be some hunting lodges in the area. If we're lucky one of them might still be standing."

"That doesn't sound very promising."

"Just keeping with the theme."

"How far?"

"Don't know exactly."

"If you don't know, how will we find it?"

"Don't know that, either."

"Cutter, if these men have access to a chopper, as far as we know they'll be waiting for us when we get there."

He looked around, gauging the snow-fall. It was coming down hard. Visibility had dwindled. The wind was whipping. "You got to be able to see to fly a chopper. Not even The Jaguar is crazy enough to fly in this mess."

A low rumble shook the earth. An instant later a helicopter roared out of the valley like a monstrous pterodactyl. The blades kicked snow into a blinding white swirl. Cutter caught a glimpse of yellow paint and black lettering. He reached for his sidearm, realized too late it wasn't there.

Shoving his prisoner toward the deer trail, he shouted, "Run! Take cover!"

They were midway to the trailhead when the first gunshot split the air.

Chapter Four

The snow and wind blinded her. Mattie didn't know if the skies had finally opened up or if the swirling snow was from the rotor blades of the chopper. All she cared about was dodging a bullet.

The endeavor seemed hopeless with the chopper hovering just a dozen yards above and two men with rifles taking potshots at them. The pines provided some cover but not enough. Over the roar of wind and engines, she could hear bullets ricocheting off rocks. She could practically feel the crosshairs of the rifles on her back and tried not to imagine what it would be like to die out here at the hands of a madman.

Cutter led her down the deer trail. They plowed through snow that was now several inches deep. Jagged rock blew past. Trees tore at her clothes. All the while she imagined the paralyzing pain of a bullet slamming into her back.

Fatigue set in quickly, the high altitude tearing down her endurance. Mattie ran as fast as she could, but it wasn't enough. Lungs and legs burning, she slowed.

Cutter gripped her hand hard. "Come on, damn it!"

"I'm trying."

"You're going to have to try harder."

Her foot hit something buried beneath the snow. Her hand was jerked from his as she tried to break her fall. She plowed facedown into three inches of snow.

"Get up!"

Mattie scrambled to her feet, but her legs were shaking violently; she didn't think she could continue running. "I don't think we're going to outrun that chopper," she shouted.

. "What do you suggest? That we give up and let them shoot us down?"

He had a point. But the situation seemed hopeless. They couldn't continue at this pace. Mattie was beyond exhaustion.

Still, he tugged her into a run. Within minutes she noticed his pace had slowed as well; she wasn't the only one who'd reached the limit of her endurance. How could the situation possibly get any worse?

Her question was answered when the trail abruptly ended at a jut of rock that shot two hundred feet straight up. For several interminable seconds they stood there, their breaths spewing into the cold air.

The moment was broken when a bullet ricocheted off a rock less than a foot from Cutter's face. "Son of a bitch," he muttered, wiping blood from his cheek.

"We're trapped," Mattie shouted, trying to stay calm, trying to think.

The chopper passed overhead. Too loud. Too close. The engine roared as it prepared to make another pass. This time she didn't think they'd miss. At least not Cutter. They had other plans for her that weren't nearly as expedient as a bullet in the heart.

"What do we do now?" she cried.

Cutter was looking down at the ground. Mattie didn't understand what he could possibly be thinking. They were sitting ducks here. They had to move! She could hear the chopper getting closer. Then Cutter motioned toward a pile of rocks twenty yards away. Her gaze followed his point. She caught a glimpse of tiny hoof marks in the snow.

"This way!" He reached for her hand.

But she pulled back. "It's a dead end!"

A volley of shots erupted. A hole blew through the sleeve of Cutter's shirt. His body jolted. Mattie saw blood and smoke and heard herself scream. The next thing she knew he locked his hand around her arm and shoved her hard enough to make her stumble. Terrified that they were about to become pinned, she started to fight him. Then she spotted the black hole in the rock face of the cliff.

"It's a cave!" he shouted. "Go!"

She didn't have to be told twice. She scrambled over rock slick with snow and ice and into the protective cloak of darkness. It was like walking into the darkest of nights. Mattie could still hear the chopper's engine. But the gunshots had stopped.

In the dim light, she saw Cutter sink to the floor of the cave. "That was damn close," he muttered.

Remembering the bullet that had torn through his shirt, she stepped closer. In the dim light she could see the dark stain of blood. "My God. You've been shot."

He glanced down at the wound. A bitter sound that was part growl, part laugh, squeezed from his throat. "I guess I have."

"Maybe I should take a look—"

"It'll keep." He reached into his belt

and slid what looked like some type of baton from his belt. Using one hand, he snapped it in two. Yellow light filled the cave. "Emergency flare," he said.

"Handy."

"I like to be prepared."

"Boy Scout, huh?"

"Something like that."

Yeah, and you're no ordinary cop, she thought as she took in the cave. The flare projected light only about ten feet. But it was far enough for her to see that the interior was narrow and damp and barely high enough for them to stand. Stones and loose dirt comprised the floor. The rock walls dripped with water.

"Not exactly The Ritz," she muttered.

"Pretty damn good for stopping bullets, though."

The mention of bullets made her shiver. "What if those men land the chopper and come after us?"

"No place to land."

"How do you—"

"Because my pilot had one hell of a time finding a decent area for the rendezvous point."

"Does that mean we're going to be okay?"

"That means this cave bought us some time."

"How much?"

When he didn't answer she glanced at him. He'd risen and was holding the flare in front of him, trying to see farther into the cave.

"Where does it lead?" she asked.

"Hopefully not to the den of some hibernating grizzly."

She squinted into the inky darkness. "You're kidding, right?"

He didn't smile, but she thought she saw a glint of amusement in his eyes. "Deer wouldn't use the cave if it was occupied by any kind of predator."

"What if it's a dead end? What if we're trapped? What if we reach the end of the cave and have to turn around? And when we do The Jaguar's men are waiting for us?"

He shot her a sharp look she didn't quite understand at the mention of The Jaguar. Reaching into his belt, he retrieved a tiny box. Only after he'd struck a match did she realize what he was doing.

"It's not a dead end," he said.

In the flickering light of the match, she noted the tension in the set of his shoulders. She wondered if he was in pain from the gunshot wound or worried that there was no escape.

"How do you know?" she asked.

"There's a draft." He held the match higher. The tiny flame danced. "See?"

"That means there's an exit?" she asked.

"The question is how far." The flame burned close to his fingers, and he swished out the match.

"And what might be waiting for us on the other end," she added.

"Only one way to find out," he said, and started into the darkness.

CUTTER DIDN'T LIKE admitting it, but he'd suffered with claustrophobia since his disastrous mission in Africa two years ago. He'd learned to live with it for the most part. He'd learned to control the slick fear the way he controlled everything else. He'd passed the psych test for entry into the MIDNIGHT team not because he'd answered the questions truthfully, but because he'd known which answers the shrinks had wanted to hear.

As he and his prisoner made their way through the snaking tunnel, he couldn't shake the feeling that they were traveling deeper and deeper into the bowels of the earth. After twenty minutes of walking, he struck a second match. A quiver of uncertainty went through him when the flame did not flicker. Had they somehow missed a turnoff that would take them out of the cave?

"What is it?"

He jolted at the sound of her voice, quickly corrected his response and schooled his features into a cool mask. "Nothing," he said.

But her eyes lingered on his a little too long, and he had to remind himself of just how important it was for him to remain in control of the situation.

"No air movement," she said.

"You let me worry about that."

For an hour the only sound came from their shoes against the rocky floor and the incessant drip of water. Cutter knew it was the claustrophobia, but he felt as if he couldn't get enough oxygen into his lungs. Soon his fingers and face began to tingle. He tried to occupy his mind with more important things—like how the hell they were going to get to a phone once they found their way out of this godfor-saken hole. But he couldn't suppress the terrible sensation of being trapped and slowly suffocated.

After a while he began to sweat. Not the kind of sweat that stemmed from physical exertion or heat—the temperature inside the cave hovered just above freezing. The sweat beading on his forehead and the back of his neck was panic sweat, and it felt like ice against his skin.

"Are you all right?"

The sound of her voice jerked him from a place he knew better than to venture. The first thing any agent learned about controlling fear when he couldn't control his environment was to discipline his mind. Not think about it. Certainly not dwell on it.

"I'm fine," he growled.

"You're breathing hard."

Ignoring her, Cutter continued walking.

Evidently, Mattie Logan wasn't the kind of woman to be ignored. Jogging to keep up with his long stride, she came up beside him and looked closely at him. "Cutter, you're sweating."

"Yeah, well, that happens when I walk ten damn miles."

"It's cold. You shouldn't be sweating like that." When he didn't answer, she bit her lip. "How bad is that bullet wound?"

The graze in his arm where the bullet had nicked him hadn't even crossed his mind. He was too busy thinking about the walls closing in. The lack of oxygen. The ceiling coming down to crush them both….

"I'm fine, damn it."

"Cutter, you're shaking. You can barely hold the flare."

For the first time he noticed just how badly he was shaking. If he didn't get a handle on the fear slithering through him, he was going to collapse into a heap on the floor like some kind of a blathering idiot.

"Let me—" She wrapped her hand around his arm as she reached for the flair. "Oh my God. You're soaking wet and trembling."

"I'm fine," he snapped. "Get away."

"Let me help you."

He shook off her hand. "I don't need your damn help."

"Look, I know you don't trust me. Frankly, I'd rather go it alone, too. We don't exactly have the same goal here. But for your information I'm not cold-blooded enough to leave you alone when you're obviously injured."

"I'm not injured."

"You look like you're ready to pass out."

At that moment Cutter figured he'd rather do just that than lose it in front of a prisoner. Unfortunately, succumbing to unconsciousness wasn't an option if he wanted to get through this. He was going to have to tough it out and hope the panic attack abated.

But the walls and ceiling continued to close in. He could feel the crushing pressure of a thousand tons of rock. The sensation of being trapped. Cold darkness descending. No oxygen to breathe.

Bending at the hip, Cutter put his hands on his knees and gulped air. He knew better than to turn his back on a prisoner, but he was in no condition to stop her if she decided to do something stupid…like run.

He could hear his breaths echoing off the rock walls. He was breathing too fast. Too shallowly. Still, he couldn't seem to get enough into his lungs.

"Cutter…"

He started when she touched him. He knew that was the one thing he should not allow. But at that moment the small human contact, the warmth of her hand against his shoulder, was incredibly reassuring.

Closing his eyes tightly, he clung to that tiny connection. After a few minutes the fear loosened its death grip. The walls and ceiling of the cave stopped closing in. His breathing returned to normal. The sweat cooled on his skin. All the while he was keenly aware of the warmth of her hand against his shoulder.

"Better." He straightened and turned to look at her. In the dim light of the flare he saw wide blue eyes and porcelain skin. Her hand fell away from his arm, and he was suddenly keenly aware of the absence of her touch. Against his will, his eyes went to her mouth, her full, pink mouth, and suddenly he remembered the kiss they'd shared. He acknowledged the fact that he wanted to do it again.

"I'm glad you're all right," she said. "For a second I thought you were going to pass out."

"I'm fine," he growled.

Two feet separated them. She was at least a foot shorter, and he had to look down to maintain eye contact. He could see the swell of her breasts. The fragile slant of her throat. In the dim light her skin looked almost translucent. The lemon and rosemary scent of her hair titillated his senses. He knew better than to want when it came to this woman, but he did. He wanted like he hadn't wanted for a long time.

The flare chose that moment to burn out, plunging them into darkness. Cutter tossed the spent stick to the ground, not sure if he was relieved the strange moment had passed or disappointed because they were going to have to travel the rest of the way in total darkness.

"Do you have another flare?" she asked.

"Nope."

"How are we going to find the other opening without light?"

Cutter struck a match. Relief flicked through him when the flame danced. "We follow the air."

"There's a breeze?"

"Faint, but definitely there." He could feel her gaze on him, but he didn't look at her. The situation demanded he either tie her belt to his or take her hand so they didn't get separated. Considering the way he was reacting to her, he didn't want to touch her. But since he was fresh out of rope he was going to have to take her hand. "Let's go."

He reached down to take her hand. She tried to tug away, but he tightened his grip. "We don't want to get separated," he explained.

"Oh." She stopped trying to pull away.

Refusing to acknowledge just how good her hand felt in his, Cutter extinguished the match and they ventured deeper into the cave.

Chapter Five

Mattie had never been afraid of the dark. Even as a child, she'd never needed a night-light or the door to her room left ajar. But the utter darkness of the cave was something she had never encountered.

She didn't know how long they walked. It seemed like hours, but the darkness had a way of skewing one's sense of time and place. If not for the warmth of Cutter's hand, she wasn't sure she would have been able to go on.

"Stop." His voice broke through the utter silence like a shout.

"What is it?" She squinted, but saw nothing.

A match flared. Relief went through her at the sight of the tiny light. Then she noticed that the flame was flickering wildly.

"We're close to the opening," Cutter said.

"I don't see any light ahead."

"The opening may be hidden. In fact, we may have to dig our way out of here."

"I hate to tell you this, but I left my shovel in my other purse."

He scowled. "Ha, ha."

"So how do we find the opening?"

"Follow the breeze."

The match burned out. He immediately lit another. "I'm going to let go of your hand. I want you to stay put."

Mattie nodded, but already it seemed her hand had grown cold without his. She stood there as he moved along the far side of the cave. He held the match with one hand, ran his other along the stone wall.

The match burned down, once again plunging them into darkness. This time, he didn't light another. Several minutes passed. Mattie could hear him moving around. She took comfort in that, but the dark and cold were beginning to get to her. She thought she heard the squeak of some type of animal. She detected a faint but foul odor and began to imagine the skeletons of long-dead explorers who'd been unable to find their way out, their bodies eaten by carnivorous rats....

A hand on her shoulder made her jump. She spun, reached out, found her hand on a hard-as-rock bicep. "Don't sneak up on me like that," she said.

"I found the opening."

She wanted to get out of the smelly, dark and damp cave and into the daylight. "Thank God. Let's get out of here."

"There's only one small problem," Cutter said.

"Believe me, there's no problem big enough to keep me from leaving this god-forsaken cave."

"I want you to stay calm," he said.

Mattie got a prickly sensation on the

back of her neck. "I'll be a lot calmer if you'd tell me why you're telling me to be calm."

Yellow light flared when Cutter struck a match. His eyes were already on hers. She gazed back at him, wondering why he was wasting time, not to mention matches. Then movement on the ceiling snagged her attention. At first she thought the soil and rock were somehow shifting. Then she realized what she was looking at were thousands of tiny bodies squeezed together to form a single, undulating layer.

Bats.

"Oh my God."

"Don't make a sound," Cutter said.

The logical part of her brain knew bats were harmless for the most part. But their small rodent bodies gave her the creeps nonetheless. "Please tell me they're not blocking our exit."

"We're going to have to walk beneath them."

Mattie closed her eyes tightly, her imagination conjuring images of sharp bat teeth sinking to skin in search of blood. "Are they vampire bats?"

"They eat insects. And they're hibernating. We should try not to disturb them."

"Cutter, I think that's one thing you're not going to have to worry about."

Amusement glinted in his eyes before the match went out. "I want you to stay with me."

She started when he took her hand. "How far is the opening?"

"Twenty feet. We go past the bats. Then we climb." He squeezed her hand. "Let's go."

The ammonia smell of guano filled her nostrils as they neared the bats. Mattie could hear the intermittent squeaks of the animals. The swish of tiny wings. The occasional spatter of droppings hitting the cave floor. Gooseflesh rose all over her body as they sidled past.

Then she felt a gust of cold, fresh air on her face. Ahead she caught a glimpse of daylight. Relief rippled through her. She let go of Cutter's hand and quickened her step. The cave narrowed, but she didn't care. All she cared about was getting out of there.

"Nice and slow," Cutter said.

But Mattie was already on her hands and knees, crawling toward the light. Sharp rocks cut uncomfortably into her knees, but she barely felt the pain. "I'm almost there," she said, excitedly.

"I'm right behind you."

She was so relieved to be out of the cave, she barely noticed when her hands plunged into snow or when cold wind slapped her face. Then the bitter cold began to permeate her clothing as she got to her feet, shivering, blinking at the bright white light.

Cutter scrambled to his feet beside her. "Out of the frying pan and into the fire," he muttered.

The lightly falling snow had burgeoned into a blizzard.

"WHAT DO WE DO NOW?"

The same question reverberated in Cutter's head as he assessed the conditions. Wind-driven snow slashed down from a white-on-white sky. Visibility was less than twenty feet. The wind had picked up markedly and blew with the wicked howl of a gale.

Under different circumstances the answer would have been clear. Stay in the cave until conditions improved. But with The Jaguar and his men in hot pursuit— possibly even inside the cave and tracking them at this very moment—Cutter knew they had no choice but to risk traveling in the storm. What it boiled down to, he realized, was how he preferred to die. Of hypothermia? Or at the hands of a man whose penchant for cruelty Cutter had already experienced once.

"We keep moving," Cutter said.

She blinked rapidly as snow swirled around her face. "How do you propose we do that when we can't see? When we have no earthly idea where we are?"

"I've got a compass."

"A compass? It's going to take a hell of a lot more than a compass to get us through this storm."

He jammed a thumb in the direction of the cave. "Or maybe you want to hang out in the cave a little while longer."

"Look, I'm no fan of vampires, but—"

"I'm not talking about the damn bats. I'm talking about The Jaguar and his men."

She looked uneasily toward the black hole from which they'd just emerged. "You think they followed us?"

"I think it's an assumption we have to make if we want to stay alive."

"If they followed us into that bat-infested cave, who's to say they won't follow us into the blizzard?"

"Knowing The Jaguar, he will." Cutter looked around. "We'll just have to make it a little more difficult for them."

He'd been saving the two concussion grenades in his belt for emergencies. This wasn't exactly an emergency, but if he could keep The Jaguar's men from following them, the small explosives would be well worth using. Tugging one of the tiny canisters from his belt, he walked over to the cave opening and looked into the darkness.

Mattie came up beside him. "What are you doing?"

"Buying us some time." He lifted the canister, set the timer, and began to silently count. *One one thousand. Two one thousand.* "See that copse of trees?" he asked, motioning toward a protected area high on the other side of the small gorge where they were standing.

She squinted. "Barely."

"You have fifteen seconds to get there. Start running. I'm right behind you."

She shot him a startled look he might have enjoyed had the circumstances not been so dire. "Why fifteen seconds?"

Aiming carefully, he tossed the grenade onto a ledge directly above them that was piled high with snow. "Because there's going to be an avalanche."

The explosion shook the earth. Cutter prayed his calculations were correct. If they weren't, he and Mattie would be buried alive by a thousand tons of churning, crushing snow.

He held on to her hand with a death grip as he dashed toward the stand of aspen trees. The ground beneath his feet trembled. He sensed the awesome power of the avalanche. Felt the spray of snow on his face.

But he didn't risk looking back. One wrong move could mean a fall. A fall at this point would mean certain death, and he had absolutely no intention of dying.

As suddenly as the explosion began, it eerily stopped. Cutter and Mattie reached the trees and higher ground. Cutter swung around. The avalanche and snowstorm had combined forces and turned the mountain into a surreal scene that was white on white on white. It was one of the most stunning sights he'd ever seen in his life.

"I can't believe you did that."

Grinning, he looked at Mattie. Her eyes were on his, midnight blue against milky skin. "Mother Nature put on a hell of a show, didn't she?"

"She's not too careful with her audience." But her gaze was fixed on the powder snow swirling down like a white tornado.

Cutter released her hand and stepped back. "That ought to hold them for a while."

"Now we can freeze to death in peace."

He frowned at her. Snow sparkled in her hair and on her skin. Her cheeks blushed with cold. Damn, he really wished she didn't look so good. If he wasn't careful, she was going to get to him on a level he didn't want to acknowledge.

"We need to keep moving." Pulling the compass from his pocket, he motioned toward the faint trail.

"Where are we going?"

"To see if we can find one of those cabins I was telling you about."

"The ones you were hoping are still standing?"

"Those are the ones."

"How far?"

"A couple of miles at most."

She gave him a sharp look. "In case you haven't noticed, we're not wearing coats."

But Cutter had noticed. He hadn't missed the fact that she was shivering. That her teeth were beginning to chatter. With nothing more than their street clothes to keep them warm, he knew it wouldn't be long before hypothermia set in.

Because she wasn't moving fast enough, he took her arm and pulled her into a brisk walk. He was starting to get cold, as well. His hands and feet were cold. To make matters worse, the throbbing of his ribs had returned with a vengeance.

Mattie had fallen silent. Cutter figured

that was just as well. He didn't want to talk to her. He didn't have the answers she wanted to hear. Finding a cabin in these conditions was going to take nothing short of a miracle. He figured they had a couple of hours before serious hypothermia set in and their bodies began shutting down.

Once that happened, their fate would be sealed.

Chapter Six

Mattie didn't know how she kept going. The cold was zapping not only her physical strength but her will to continue. It took every bit of her concentration just to put one foot in front of the other. She was beyond cold. Beyond exhaustion. Her hands were numb. Her feet felt like solid ice and ached every time they touched the ground. The urge to collapse and simply give up was strong. But Mattie had never been a quitter.

Ahead Cutter trudged through deep snow. He was like a machine set on auto-pilot, moving forward at a steady rate. She didn't know how he did it. She was growing more exhausted with each step. Her arms were sluggish. Her legs felt weighted down. Even though she was moving, sleepiness tugged at her. In her peripheral vision the trees and snow blurred into a solid gray mass.

They'd just reached the valley floor when she fell. One moment she was slogging along, thinking about a hot shower and a warm bed, the next she was lying facedown on the ground. The snow was cold against her face but at least she could rest now. She curled more deeply into the snow and closed her eyes….

"Mattie, come on. Get up."

The voice came to her as if from a great distance. She knew it was Cutter. She knew he wanted her to get up. Didn't he understand that she needed to rest? She hadn't the strength to argue with him. She just wanted him to leave her alone.

The next thing she knew he'd hauled her to her feet. "Get up," he growled. "I'm not going to let you do this."

"Tired," she muttered, surprised when she slurred the word.

"I know you're tired. So am I. But we can't stop now."

"Gotta rest," she murmured. "Just…a little while."

The gentle slap of his palm against her cheek roused her. Mattie glared at him, a sharp retort on her tongue. But for the life of her she couldn't manage the words. All she wanted to do was sleep….

"You're going into hypothermia," he said. "Damn it, you've got to keep moving."

Mattie tried to take a step forward, just to appease him, but one knee buckled and she went down. Her hands were covered in snow. Oddly, they were no longer cold. The knees of her slacks were wet against her skin. But the snow looked so inviting. "Leave me 'lone."

"Not a chance."

The next thing she knew she was being dragged up and into his arms. She wasn't so far gone that it didn't register in her mind that she was too heavy for him to carry in his deteriorated condition. But she was too weak to argue.

Warmth emanated from his body into hers. Mattie relaxed against him. She felt her head loll back. She looked up at the swirling gray sky, caught a glimpse of Cutter's face. His lips had a blue tinge, but his jaw was set, his expression was determined.

He's saving my life, she thought dazedly.

Then darkness descended in a cold black rush, and she didn't think of anything at all.

FAILURE WAS THE ONE THING The Jaguar could not tolerate. Not in himself. Certainly not when it came to others. But that was exactly what had happened. His team had failed him. Which meant *he* had failed.

Holed up in a tourist hotel twenty miles from the Canadian border and waiting out the storm, he was not in a good mood.

He'd never been good at waiting. He'd never been a good sport when it came to losing. Or when it came to failing. He would *not* let the American scientist slip from his grasp.

"How did this happen?" he asked, his voice not betraying the fury building inside him.

"We followed them into the cave. We were minutes away from apprehending them, but an avalanche blocked the cave exit." The young man's glossy black hair was swept back in a ponytail revealing high cheekbones and heavy brows. His eyes and voice were level and calm. Like all the other men who worked for The Jaguar, he was a professional. But The Jaguar saw the nervousness just beneath the surface. The way the young man's hands fluttered when he spoke. The up-and-down motion of his Adam's apple as he swallowed.

"An avalanche?"

"We believe the American agent used an explosive to set off an avalanche sealing the cave and preventing us from following."

"I see."

The young man's eyes went to the window where snow continued to fall. "Perhaps after the storm—"

The Jaguar spun on him. "Not after the storm. Now. I want the chopper fueled and ready to go in an hour."

"But the FAA has grounded all—"

The Jaguar leaned close, so that his face was mere inches from the younger man's. "Are you a coward? Afraid to die for your cause?"

"No."

"Good. Fuel the chopper. Brief the pilot. Make sure he's ready to lift off within the hour."

The young man bowed his head slightly. "Of course."

But The Jaguar wasn't finished. "Tell the rest of the men that I personally will kill any man who is not prepared to die for this cause."

The young man nodded once then turned and fled the room.

CUTTER CARRIED HER as far as he could, and then he carried her a little farther. Visibility had dwindled to zero. The wind slapped at his face like a rude, icy hand. The cold stole through his body, paralyzing his muscles.

At some point in the past hours, he'd accepted the very real possibility that they were going to die out here. The optimistic side of his mind reasoned that at least they would not die at the cruel hands of The Jaguar. Hypothermia wasn't such a bad way to go. The only problem with that logic was that Cutter wasn't ready to call it quits for at least another thirty or forty years.

But he was thinking about stopping. Just laying Mattie down in the snow, snuggling up beside her and holding her until the cold claimed them both. But then, that would be the easy way out. And he'd never been able to do things the easy way.

Just then he stumbled over something buried in the snow. Weakened by hypothermia, he dropped Mattie and fell flat on his face. For the span of several seconds he just lay there. Damn, this was bad. He should get up and do something. Maybe dig a snow shelter. At least that would get them out of the wind.

Mattie lay next to him, her hair wet, her complexion deathly pale. Dear God, had she succumbed to the cold? Shaken, he started to get up to reach for her and noticed the slow rise and fall of her chest. Thank goodness she was breathing. But he knew they couldn't last much longer. Damn, he hadn't wanted things to end this way.

He wasn't sure where he found the strength, but he got to his knees, scooped her into his arms and struggled to his feet.

That was when he realized the thing he'd stumbled over was not a log, but a piece of wood. He squinted into the blinding white swirl of the blizzard. At first he thought he was seeing some bizarre mirage. Then he realized the board had fallen off the porch of a small cabin. He'd stumbled upon the very thing he'd spent the past several hours searching for: the old hunting lodge.

Cutter stumbled onto the ramshackle porch. He rammed the front door with his shoulder. The rotting wood gave way with a resonant snap. He staggered into the murky interior. Dust and the musty odor of rotting wood filled his nostrils. Straight ahead a river-rock hearth dominated the room. Grimy windows allowed little light inside, but there was enough for him to see the rickety table and chairs near the rear door. A small sink. Cupboards. A bunk.

The woman in his arms stirred. Cutter looked down at her. "Hang on, blondie," he whispered.

He swept dust and small debris from the bunk and set her on the mattress. Looking around, he spotted a tattered blanket draped over the back of a chair. Cutter opened the blanket and covered her with it. It would have to be enough until he could get a fire started.

His head spun when he rose, and he fought to maintain his balance. He needed wood for the fire. His limbs felt as if they were made of lead as he crossed to the table and chairs. Awkwardly, he lifted one of the chairs to shoulder height, and brought it down on the table. Once. Twice. The table broke into two pieces on the third try. Another blow and two of the chair's legs clattered to the floor.

Cutter gathered the wood and stacked it neatly in the hearth. He found several pages of an ancient newspaper someone had used to line the cupboards, wadded it up and placed it beneath the wood. A curse broke from his lips when he pulled the matchbox from his pocket and found most of the matches damp. Picking through, he finally found one that was dry, struck it against the stone. It lit. Carefully he set the flame beneath the wood and watched the paper ignite.

Once the wood was burning, he turned back to Mattie. She looked incredibly small and vulnerable lying curled on her side beneath the old blanket. He had to get those wet clothes off her. Cutter didn't want to do it—he wasn't at all comfortable with the way he was responding to her—but he knew enough about hypothermia to know nothing zapped body heat more effectively than water.

Kneeling next to her, he set his hand on her shoulder. "Mattie?"

"Tired…" she muttered, but she didn't open her eyes.

"We did it," he said. "We're in the cabin. I made a fire. See? You need to get out of those wet clothes so you can get warm."

Her eyes fluttered open. She didn't seem to recognize him. Worry descended at the sight of her dilated pupils. Her core body temperature was dangerously low. She was in no condition to undress. If her heart rate and oxygen intake slowed…

"I'm going to get you out of those clothes, okay?"

"Gotta…sleep." Her words slurred.

"Not right now." Reaching behind her, he lifted her to a sitting position and glanced down at her clothes. She was still wearing the tattered black wool suit jacket and slacks. A white blouse. She was soaked to the skin.

Propping her against his right arm and shoulder, he used his left to unbutton the jacket. Mattie was like a rag doll in his arms as he worked the jacket from her body and tossed it to the floor. The blouse clung to her like skin. Beneath it, he discerned the lace of her bra and the swell of her breasts. His fingers shook as he began unbuttoning the blouse.

"Wha'r you doing?" Mattie thrashed and brushed at his hands.

Cutter didn't stop. "You've got hypothermia," he said firmly. "These wet clothes need to go so your body can warm up."

He tried not to look when her blouse fell open. But his gaze was irresistibly drawn to the swell of her generous breasts encased in lace and cotton, a flat belly and the kind of curves a man liked to sink his hands into.

She slapped at his hand. "Please. Don't."

Cutter caught her wrist. "Easy," he said. "I have to do this. Then we'll put you next to the fire, okay?"

The mention of the fire seemed to calm her. Cutter quickly removed her blouse. He tried not to touch her skin as he undid her slacks. Tried even harder not to look as he peeled the material down her long, shapely legs. But while Sean Cutter was a MIDNIGHT agent first and foremost, he was also a man.

The memory of the way her body had felt against his assailed him. The softness of her mouth. The warmth of her breath against his cheek. Not even hypothermia could keep the blood from rushing hotly to his groin….

How could he be so damn attracted to the woman he'd been hired to take back? A woman who'd betrayed her country?

Annoyed with himself, Cutter ground his teeth. Quickly, and as impersonally as possible, he removed her shoes, then her slacks. Her bra and panties were wet as well, but there was no way he was going to remove them. Covering her with the blanket, he then dragged the bunk closer to the fire so she would get maximum heat.

He hung her clothes over the back of a chair and set it next to the hearth for quick drying, then set to work removing his own wet clothing. He had begun to shiver, which was a good sign. His body was coming to life, trying to warm itself and raise his body temperature back to a normal level. But even with the fire blazing, the temperature inside the cabin was below freezing. If they were going to recover enough to walk out of there under their own power, he was going to have to do a hell of a lot better.

Aside from the fire, the next best source of warmth was body heat. As much as he didn't want to think about crawling onto that cot with Mattie Logan when they were wearing nothing more than underwear, he knew it was the smartest thing to do. Not only for him, but for her. Her body temperature was dangerously low. Warming too quickly could shunt cold blood from the surface of the body to the internal organs, causing shock. Body heat was the perfect solution.

Shivering uncontrollably, he lifted the blanket from Mattie. She was lying curled on her side. Trying not to notice her beauty, he bent and touched her shoulder with the back of his fingers. Her skin was cold to the touch, but her lips were no longer blue. He checked her pulse, found it slow. *Too slow,* he thought.

Decision made, he climbed onto the cot

and lay down behind her with his body spooning hers. Pulling the blanket over both of them, he wrapped his arm around her torso. He willed himself not to think of her in inappropriate terms, but his body had no such reservations. The mattress smelled moldy, but it was the scent of rosemary and lemon that filled his nostrils as he drifted into a dreamless sleep.

Chapter Seven

Mattie woke to blessed warmth and the sensation of a muscular male body snugged up against hers. Her first thought was that she'd just wakened from a very bad dream. She was back in her condo in D.C. She'd finally slept with Daniel. But none of those things explained why every part of her body ached. Or why the wind was howling and snow was battering the windows with the force of tiny missiles.

The urge to shut her eyes again and snuggle closer to the warm—and evidently aroused—male body was powerful. But as the fog of exhaustion-induced sleep lifted, the events of the past twenty-four hours flooded back into her brain. The crash of the prison van. The cold-blooded murders of the U.S. Marshals. Running for her life in hostile mountain terrain. The man with icy blue eyes carrying her through blizzard conditions…

Mattie sat up abruptly. The ramshackle room was cold despite the embers glowing in the hearth. Then she noticed she was wearing only her bra and panties, and as far as she could tell the man lying next to her was half-naked, as well.

She scrambled from the cot, taking the blanket with her. "What the hell do you think you're doing?" she asked.

Cutter instantly awoke and sat bolt upright. His eyes darted first to the door, then to her. "Judging from the look on your face, not what you're thinking."

Mattie couldn't help it. Of their own accord, her eyes flicked down his body. He was wearing a shirt, but it was open. She saw a muscular chest covered with swirls of black hair; a six-pack stomach that was flat and rock hard; long, athletic legs. He wore navy boxer shorts, and she couldn't help but notice he filled them out the way a man ought to fill out boxer shorts.

Banking the thoughts that were crazy at a time like this, Mattie glared at him. She'd heard of male members of law enforcement taking advantage of female prisoners. The thought had always disgusted her, frightened her if she wanted to be honest about it. Even though she didn't know him well, she couldn't imagine Cutter stooping that low. Up until this point he'd been Mr. Professional Cop. But how had she ended up half-naked and in bed with him?

"You took off my clothes," she accused.

"I removed wet clothing to keep you from losing body heat," he said. "You were hypothermic."

"You had no right."

"If I hadn't, you very likely would have died."

She motioned toward him. "Is that why you took off your clothes, too?"

He reached for the dusty pillow and set it on his lap. "You weren't the only one whose clothes were wet. We'd been in the snow for hours. We were both wet. We needed shelter and to get dry."

Mattie remembered trudging through impossibly deep snow. She remembered the terrible feeling of exhaustion and confusion and the utter certainty that she was going to die. Only then did it dawn on her that this man had saved her life. That in the scope of things, her vanity was the last thing she ought to be worried about.

"Nothing happened," he said.

"How long was I out?"

He glanced toward the window. "Judging from the light, I'd say we slept a couple of hours."

She looked into his eyes. "You saved my life."

"I did what I had to do."

"I'm sorry I assumed…" Not sure how to finish, she let the sentence dangle.

"Hypothermia can cause confusion," he said. "That's how it works. You get tired. You get confused. You lie down and never get up."

She released the breath she'd been holding. "Thank you."

"I was just doing my job."

Unable to meet his gaze, she looked out the window. Through the grime, she could see that the snow was still coming down hard. "What do we do now?"

"Rest. Find some food. Keep the fire going." He parted the shirt and glanced down at his chest, shrugged. "Both of us are pretty banged up."

Mattie caught sight of the angry red and purple bruises covering the flesh just below his left pectoral, gasping at the severity of them. "My God. Is that where you were shot back at the rendezvous point?"

He nodded. "My vest stopped the bullet,

but it sure as hell didn't keep it from cracking a rib or two."

Mattie knew how painful broken ribs could be. When she was a teenager a car accident left her with two cracked ribs. She'd been laid up for a week and missed her junior prom. She couldn't imagine having broken ribs and trudging through a blizzard. She certainly couldn't imagine how much it had hurt him to carry her.

"Wouldn't it have been easier if you'd left me behind to die?" she asked.

"My job isn't about easy most of the time."

Because she didn't know how to respond to that, Mattie pulled the blanket more tightly around her and walked to the hearth. "Looks like we're about to run out of wood," she said, motioning toward the few remaining pieces of the table he'd been using.

"There's no way we're going to find dry firewood outside. Once that wood is gone, we burn whatever we can find, including the walls of the mud room and cabinets." Rising, he walked swiftly to where his jeans hung near the hearth and stepped into them.

Mattie caught a glimpse of muscular male thighs. Lean hips encased in snug boxer shorts. The hint of a part of his anatomy she didn't want to think about…

"What about The Jaguar?" she asked.

He shot her a sharp look. He always did that, she realized, whenever she mentioned the terrorist by that name. The Jaguar had reacted much the same way when his underling had mentioned Cutter's name. She wondered if the men had some kind of history.

Grimacing, he looked out the window. "It's hard to imagine a pilot crazy enough to fly a chopper in this weather."

"If I recall, you'd just said something similar at about the time said chopper swooped down and those men started shooting at us."

"I've never been good at predicting

when someone is going to do something completely insane."

An uneasy feeling stole over her. "That means they could be on their way here at this very moment to kill us."

"They could. But they have to find us first. Then they have to get here. This area is remote."

"It'll be dark soon," she said. "That will help us, won't it? Hide us? Hide the cabin?"

"I wish I could say yes, but I can't. If they've got infrared, the fire in the hearth will stand out like a beacon. The best we can hope for is that the storm continues and they can't fly."

"Not very reassuring considering they already flew at the height of the storm."

Looking out the window, he shook his head. "If that son of a bitch is crazy enough to fly, all we can do is hope we hear them coming."

CUTTER HAD NEVER BEEN GOOD at waiting; he'd sure as hell never been good at staying idle. Especially when there was something important he needed to do— like stop a madman. But while being holed up in a dilapidated cabin was bad enough, it was infinitely worse being locked up with a woman he was attracted to.

Only, Mattie Logan wasn't just any woman. She was his prisoner. An assignment. A convicted criminal he'd been charged with apprehending and transporting to prison. How could he feel anything but disdain toward her?

Frustrated and restless, Cutter paced from the window to the door and back to the window. Usually he saw the world in stark black and white. Right and wrong. Good and evil. Things were simpler that way. Mattie Logan was a gray area somewhere in between, and she was anything but simple.

Usually he had good instincts when it came to people. Those instincts had saved his hide more times than he cared to count. So why couldn't he shake the feeling that there was more to her than met the eye? Or was it his attraction to her that was muddying the waters?

"You should let me take a look at that bullet wound."

He started at the sound of her voice and turned quickly to face her. She was standing a few feet away. Even in the semidarkness her beauty touched him in a place he didn't want reached. He saw the cut on her temple. The bruise on her cheekbone. He wasn't the only one who'd gotten banged up in the past twenty-four hours.

He wasn't sure why he wanted to argue with her, because she was right. Maybe he wasn't sure how he would react if she put those pretty hands on his body.

"I'll melt some snow so we can clean up," he heard himself say.

Ten minutes later he found her sitting on the single remaining chair next to the hearth. She looked up when he returned to the cabin carrying an old pan filled with snow.

"How long do you think this storm will last?" she asked.

"Hard to tell. It's showing no sign of abating."

"Do you think The Jaguar—"

"I don't know," he said abruptly.

She looked away but not before he saw the hurt in her eyes.

Annoyed with himself, he sighed. It was The Jaguar he was angry with; he shouldn't be taking it out of her just because she was getting to him in a way he didn't want to be gotten to.

Cutter set the pan of snow on the embers to melt. "I didn't mean to snap," he said.

She turned those eyes on him. "It's okay," she said. "The situation has made both of us tense."

Silence reigned as he shoved the pan more deeply into the fire. "I don't have a first-aid kit, so we'll boil this water, use it to get our cuts cleaned up. Hopefully, it will be enough to stave off infection."

"How long do you think it will be before someone finds us or before we can get back?"

The water had begun to boil so he pulled it from the hearth and carried it over to her. "I'm sure the agency is out looking for us as we speak."

"The Jaguar is, too, though, isn't he?"

His gaze met hers. Within the blue depths of her eyes he saw all the things he didn't want to see. Fear. A softness no one could fake. Real emotions. An innocence he didn't want to acknowledge. Cutter excelled at reading people—especially the things they didn't want him to see. That was one of the talents that made him such a good agent. The problem was he just couldn't see this woman contacting and dealing with terrorists.

"Probably," he said thickly.

"What do we do if he—"

"Look," he said harshly. "I don't know the answers to all your questions."

"I think we should have some sort of plan," she said. "You know, a worst-case scenario."

"We do have a plan."

"What is it?"

"If that son of a bitch shows up here we run like hell."

"Oh, that's brilliant."

"You got a better idea?"

"You're the secret agent here, not me."

"You're the genius scientist. You should damn well know that if you mess with fire you're going to get burned."

She stood abruptly. "Why do you hate me so much?"

"What I feel for you is not nearly as personal as hatred."

"I did not do any of what I was convicted of. If any of the police agencies that had worked my case had been able to see past their noses, they would have noticed that the case was *too* perfect. Too…airtight."

"You're not going to convince me of anything, so you may as well give it up."

"Look, Cutter, I have an IQ of 150. I graduated from high school when I was fourteen. I graduated from the University of Michigan when most of my friends were still in high school."

"So you're smart," he said. "Big deal."

"The point I'm getting at is this: if I had wanted to sell secrets to some terrorist organization, there's no way I would have left a trail of clues Helen Keller could find!"

Her words echoed within the confines of the cabin. She stared at him, her eyes wide and flashing, her nostrils flaring with each breath. And in some small, gullible corner of his brain, he wondered if she was telling the truth.

Because he didn't want to deal with that question at the moment, he dipped a clean cloth he'd torn from his shirt into the water and scrubbed it against the tiny bar of lye soap he'd found on the counter. "This might sting a little," he said.

"That's hardly of consequence when my life is totally destroyed." She winced when he set the cloth against her temple and began to gently scrub at the dried blood. The cut was deep. He could see the dark bruise rising on her pale skin. All he could think was that he hated to see such pretty skin marred.

"I was framed," she said abruptly.

Cutter's hand stilled. "And who is this mysterious person who allegedly framed you?"

"Daniel Savage," she replied. "My co-worker."

MY LOVER, a cruel little voice added.

It had taken Mattie months to figure out what had happened. How ironic that the person she'd trusted the most—a man she'd trusted with her heart, her body—would be the one to betray her.

"How do you know it was him?" Sean Cutter's gaze met hers with such intensity that for a moment Mattie had a difficult time meeting it.

"I don't know for certain," she said. "But Daniel is the only person who had access to the information—much of it highly restricted."

"What kind of information?" Cutter finished cleaning the cut on her temple and let his hand fall away.

"Everything you ever wanted to know about the EDNA Project but were afraid to ask."

"Mattie, that's not an answer."

"He accessed my laptop without my knowing it, Cutter."

"Aren't there security measures?"

"I had my ID and password taped to the bottom of my pencil drawer."

"Not too creative."

"I wasn't expecting my coworker to commit treason."

"What else?"

Feeling like a gullible fool, she looked

away. "Whoever framed me knew things only Daniel could have known."

"Like what?"

"Well, Daniel and I talked quite a bit. We were…close, you know? He was the only person I knew who was as passionate about the EDNA Project as I was. Only, now I realize that passion was about betrayal and money, not science."

She raised her gaze to his. "I trusted him and opened up to him. We brainstormed ideas. I told Daniel things I hadn't told anyone else. I shared my theories with him. I revealed my concerns that the weapons system was too powerful for the specifications DOD had laid out for us. Some of the topics we discussed were used to frame me. Tell me that does not reek of a setup."

"Topics like what?"

Even after what had been done to her by a government she had once trusted, Mattie had a difficult time talking about such top-secret matters. "This is top-secret information, Cutter."

He arched a brow. "I've got a high level security clearance."

"So did Daniel."

"Yeah, well, I'm not Daniel."

She flushed. "Okay. For example, when I'm first beginning a project, I do a lot of sketching. I had sketched some of my plans for EDNA. Diagrams. Rough stuff. Not to scale. I always figured the sketches wouldn't mean anything to anyone except me." Just remembering hurt, made her feel like a fool. Made her feel the stab of betrayal all over again. "Well, the sketches went missing."

"Someone broke into your office?"

"Nothing was broken into. Evidently, someone had the key and wanted me to think I had misplaced them." She shook her head. "I don't misplace stuff like that."

"What happened?"

"Three months later those sketches were found in the hotel room of one of the terrorists." A breath shuddered out of her. "I would never do anything so stupid."

"Smart people do stupid things sometimes when it comes to money."

"I didn't need money."

"So you say."

"Cutter, I made a good living. I was happy and satisfied with my work."

"So how did eight hundred thousand dollars find its way into your checking account?"

She stomped the quick rise of anger. "I see you did your homework."

"I always do, Mattie. I read your file."

"Then you know that throughout my trial, I maintained my innocence. I have no idea how the money got into my account."

"What else are you going to say?"

"Look, if I was going to accept money for selling secrets, you can bet I'd set up a Swiss account or an account in the Cayman Islands at the very least. I wouldn't deposit it into my personal account."

Cutter stared hard at her, studying her reactions, her body language, her ability to maintain eye contact with him. Everything about her said that she was telling the truth. As unlikely as it seemed, was it possible she'd been framed? Or was the keen attraction he felt for her skewing his judgment?

The last time his hormones had gotten involved when he was on assignment, someone had ended up dead. He'd nearly ended up dead himself. And to this day he couldn't look at the scars on his body and not shiver with horror.

"The feds are not stupid, Mattie," he said.

"No, but it was an election year and in a post 9/11 world, they were under intense pressure to find the culprit and bring them to justice." She blew out a pent-up breath. "They didn't look any harder than they had to, Cutter. It was all right there. Neatly planted. Motive. Means. Opportunity. Like a puzzle a five-year-old child could solve. All they had to do was put the pieces together."

He wasn't sure which was worse, believing that this lovely, angel-faced woman was guilty of treason. Or entertaining the possibility that she'd endured a trial and spent four months in prison for a crime she hadn't committed.

"I don't care if you believe me or not," she said.

The hurt and hopelessness in her eyes told him otherwise. "Look, when we get back," he heard himself say, "I'll make some inquiries."

"You'll look into it?"

"I'm not making any promises, but I'll take another look at your file. At the transcripts. I'll make a few calls. See if I can come up with anything."

"I don't know what to say." Choking back a sound that was part laugh, part sob, she blinked back tears. "Thank you."

"Don't thank me," he said. "I'm not doing this for you."

"Then why—"

"If you're innocent, then the person

who sold those secrets to The Jaguar is still out there. We both know it's only a matter of time before he does it again."

Chapter Eight

"You're going to have to let me take a look at that bullet wound." The last thing Mattie wanted to do was clean up a bloody bullet wound, but she figured they both knew that once they left the cabin they likely wouldn't get another chance.

Cutter glanced her way from his sentry post at the window. "It'll keep."

"It bled a lot."

"It's only a graze."

"Grazes get infected, too." She could tell by his expression that he knew she was right.

Looking none too happy at the prospect of her administering first aid, he crossed to the chair near the fire and sat down. "Fine. If it will make you happy, take a look."

"What will make me happy is getting off this godforsaken mountain so I can clear my name and get my life back."

He watched her as she crossed to him, and Mattie felt a tinge of self-consciousness. He had the most penetrating stare of any person she'd ever met.

"I know it's cold in here, but you're going to have to take off your shirt," she said.

His expression was impassive as his fingers worked the buttons of his flannel shirt. But rather than remove it, he simply opened it.

All thoughts about bullet wounds and terrorists and clearing her name fled the instant his chest loomed into view. Mattie had seen plenty of male chests in her thirty-one years, but she had never seen one as perfect as Sean Cutter's. It was a work of art carved into stone by an artisan with an eye for male beauty.

"So am I going to live?" he asked.

His words drew her from her momentary stupor. Mattie reached out and slid one side of the shirt down his injured shoulder. The sight of the wound made her gasp. The bullet had cut a jagged, two-inch-long path through his flesh. The surrounding skin was the color of eggplant and covered with dried blood.

"If this is a graze, I'd hate to see your idea of a serious wound," she said.

"I've had my tetanus shot."

"What about rabies?"

"I don't bite." His smile was wan. "Most of the time, anyway."

"That remains to be seen."

The wound was on his left triceps. Raising his arm, he looked at it. "All we can do now is scrub it clean and hope infection doesn't set in."

Her hands trembled as she reached for the lye soap. She dipped the tiny bar into the water, worked up some lather and then set her fingers against the wound. "Hurt?" she asked.

"What do you think?"

"I think that was probably a silly question."

When she began to rub her fingertips against the wound in small, circular motions, she could feel his muscles tightening. She knew the soap was stinging the wound, that the pressure she was applying was causing pain. But there was no way around it, so she continued with the cleansing.

"Tell me about Daniel Savage."

She froze for an instant. "He was my coworker."

"Was he your boss?"

"I was his boss."

He nodded. "Were you friends?"

"Yes."

"Were you more than friends?"

"Yes," she said after a moment.

"Okay."

She didn't know what he meant by that

simple acknowledgment, but she wasn't going to elaborate. She didn't want to talk about Daniel or just how big a fool she'd been to let him into her heart.

"Do you have any proof he set you up, or is your theory conjecture?"

"My theory is based on logic. I've had a lot of time to think about everything that happened. Cutter, I'm sure of it. Every piece of evidence that was used against me points to him." She sighed and was surprised to hear a shudder. "I think your graze is as clean as it's going to get."

"Thanks." Grimacing, he pulled his shirt back over his shoulder and glanced toward the window. "Looks like the storm may be letting up."

Relieved to be off the subject of Daniel, Mattie followed his gaze. The snow was still coming down, but not as heavily. She could still hear the wind, but it no longer shook the walls. "Do you think we can travel?"

"I think we should try to get some

sleep. If the weather continues to im-
prove, we'll take off in a few hours."

EVEN THOUGH Mattie was exhausted,
sleep refused to come. She lay a few feet
from the hearth on the scratchy blanket
and stared into the low-burning embers,
trying not to think about the state of her
life. Outside, the wind no longer howled,
but she could still hear it whispering
through the cracks of the old cabin. The
patter of snow against the windows had
slacked, but she could still see it falling
beyond the dirty glass.

She'd just begun to drift when a sound
from across the room jerked her awake.
It was the kind of sound an injured animal
made while in the throes of death.
Alarmed, she sat up and looked around.
In the dim light from the fire she could
see Cutter lying on the floor a few feet
away. She was about to call out to him
when she realized he was the source of
the sound.

It came again. Part moan, part scream, the sound was fraught with pain and terror. It was a hopeless sound filled with resignation and suffering. The kind of sound that made her want to put her hands over her ears.

She saw his body jerk. Once. Twice. A moan wrenched from his throat. "Monique," he groaned. "Aw, God...Monique..." He muttered something in French.

Not sure if he was in the throes of a nightmare or if he'd developed a fever from the bullet wound, Mattie rose and went to him. "Cutter?"

He moved so quickly she didn't have time to react. One moment she was bent over him, touching his shoulder, concerned that he was delirious with fever, the next she was lying on her back with the blade of a knife pressed to her throat.

He stared down at her for a full five seconds before blinking. She could see him pulling himself back. Cursing, he shook himself, then got to his feet and walked over to the window to lean against the sill.

Mattie lay on her back, her heart pounding, unable to believe what had just happened. Something horrific had been released inside him. Something that didn't have anything to do with the bullet wound or fever or even the situation. He'd thought she was someone else. Someone he'd wanted to kill. She'd seen the surprise in his eyes the instant he'd recognized her. The flash of regret. The realization that he'd been out of control and about to cross a line.

Slowly Mattie got to her feet. "What the hell was that all about?"

"Don't ever do that again," he ground out.

"Do what? Show concern?"

Cutter braced his arms against the sill. "I don't need your concern."

"You cried out in your sleep. I thought you'd developed a fever. I was trying to help."

"I don't need your help."

Mattie touched her throat where the blade had been pressed. Anger joined the chorus of shock and fear when she looked at her fingertip and saw blood. Her hands and legs trembled as she walked over to him. "You came within an inch of cutting my throat."

"I didn't."

"Yes, you did." She thrust her fingers at him.

His eyes flicked to the blood. Remorse filled his gaze. "I'm sorry. I thought you were…someone else."

"Who?"

"It was a dream," he said. "Let it go."

"It was more than a dream, Cutter. It was a nightmare. You were covered with sweat and crying out in your sleep."

Straightening, he turned to her. "Mattie, this is not your concern. Let it go."

"It is my business when I have to worry about you mistaking me for someone else and cutting my throat."

When he raked a hand through his short-cropped hair, Mattie saw his whole arm was trembling. What had upset this seemingly unflappable man so completely?

"Cutter, you're shaking."

"It's damn cold." He sent her a scathing look. "What the hell do you expect?"

"The truth would be a nice place to start."

He gave a small, bitter laugh and looked away. "Coming from you that's almost funny."

Mattie let the jab roll off her. "You called out a name in your sleep," she said.

His shoulders went rigid. A man made of stone and about to crumble, was all she could think.

"Monique," she said. "You were speaking in French."

Turning away from her, he strode to the window and looked out at the lightly falling snow.

"Who was she?" she asked.

"I don't know anyone by that name. Never have."

But Mattie knew he was lying. And she knew that whoever Monique was, she'd had a tremendous effect on this man. That the relationship hadn't ended well.

"Does this have something to do with The Jaguar?" she asked.

His eyes were hard when he faced her, all traces of emotion wiped clean. "The storm has broken," he said. "Gather your things. We need to leave."

"You're not going to talk about this, are you?"

"No." Turning away from her, he began to gather a few scant items.

Sighing, Mattie glanced out the window. The prospect of going back out into the cold and snow sent a shudder through her. "We don't have gear for hiking in this kind of weather. We don't even have coats."

Cutter walked to the blanket lying on

the floor. Kneeling beside it, he withdrew his knife and began cutting it.

"Why are you cutting up our only blanket?"

"I'm making you a poncho."

"Are you going to make me breakfast and a pair of boots, too?"

"Maybe next time." Rising, he crossed to her and placed the poncho over her head. She jumped when he reached out and lifted her hair out of the collar.

"Good color on you," he said thickly.

"I've always looked good in dusty old blankets."

He didn't smile, but there was a flash of amusement in his eyes.

The distinct sound of a chopper shattered the moment. Cutter jolted, rushed to the window. "Son of a bitch," he hissed.

"Please tell me that's someone coming to rescue us." But from the look on Cutter's face she knew it was not the case.

"Get out!" he shouted, running toward her. "Run! Now!"

Grabbing her hand, he jerked her hard toward the door. They were midway through it when the cabin exploded.

twenty feet away as still as death. It wasn't the first time Cutter had seen death. He'd crossed paths with the grim reaper too many times to count. But there was something obscene about seeing her small body twisted and still.

"Aw, no," he heard himself say. "Mattie…"

The world went into slow motion as he rushed toward her. All he could think was that there was a very good possibility she was innocent. That her safety had been his responsibility. Now her death was his responsibility as well, and it was a load Cutter was not equipped to bear.

He went to his knees beside her. Gently he rolled her onto her back. In the distance he was aware of the chopper's engines and the *whop! whop! whop!* of the blades as the craft drew nearer. Even without looking he knew the pilot was lining up to fire another rocket.

But he couldn't tear his eyes away from Mattie. A crimson line ran from the corner of her mouth to her cheek. Oh dear God no…

Knowing they would soon be in full view of the gunner, Cutter scooped her into his arms and struggled to his feet. He looked over his shoulder, spotted the chopper hovering a hundred yards away. Wind and snow pelted him. He could practically feel the crosshairs burning into his back…

Her body was warm and soft against his as he scrambled toward the tree line twenty yards away. He was midway there when the second rocket exploded. The concussion slapped him in the back like a giant hand. Snow and debris bombarded him. He did his best to protect Mattie, but his main concern was getting them to cover. More than likely the next missile would not miss its mark.

A bullet ricocheted off the trunk of an aspen. The sound of automatic rifle fire exploded all around. A second bullet whizzed past his right ear, close enough for him to hear its deadly zing.

He heard the *thwack! thwack! thwack!* as bullets penetrated trees and the earth. He ran until his legs gave out. At the bottom of a ravine where a frozen stream wound through boulders the size of pickup trucks, he fell to his knees. His chest heaved. Gently he set Mattie on the ground and concentrated on getting oxygen into his lungs.

"Cutter?"

His heart skipped when he looked down at her and found her eyes on him. Relief and another emotion he didn't want to identify jammed his throat as she struggled to a sitting position and looked around.

"What happened?"

"Just take it easy," he heard himself say.

"My head." She reached up and touched the back of her head. "Ouch."

He scooted over to her and for a moment all he could do was stare. "Are you all right?" he asked.

"I haven't decided." Her brows knitted in pain and she focused on him. "What happened?"

"They hit the cabin with a rocket."

"A rocket? Seems like overkill, don't you think?"

"Guess they wanted to be thorough." Cutter grimaced. "They waited until we were out. They want you alive, Mattie."

Her eyes were large and frightened when they met his. Cutter stared at her, emotions he had no business feeling churning in his gut. "Let me take a look at your head."

She pulled the ponytail holder from her hair. "I don't think it's cut."

"Whatever hit you knocked you out cold." He set his hand against her scalp. The bump was the size of a hen's egg. "No cut," he said, but didn't remove his hand.

"Feels like my head exploded."

Her hair was like silk beneath his fingertips. Unable to stop himself, he ran his fingers through it. But suddenly a chaste touch wasn't enough.

"I'm glad you're all right," he said thickly.

"'All right' being a relative state at this point." She shot him a questioning look when he cupped the side of her face.

Cutter knew he was about to make a mistake. He knew by kissing her he would be taking a very big step over a line he swore he would never cross. Once he got a taste of her mouth, he would only want more. But with the remnants of fear and adrenaline running hot in his veins, it was a risk he found himself willing to take.

Leaning close, he set his mouth against hers. Her quick intake of breath told him he'd surprised her, but he didn't stop, and she didn't pull away. He ran his tongue along the seam of her lips, seeking entry. His heart beat hard against his ribs. Blood rushed hotly to his groin. He wanted to put his arms around her. He wanted her body against his. Wanted his body inside hers…

The sound of rotors whipping the air jerked him back to reality. He pulled away. Her expression was startled. He wanted to say something, or maybe apologize for crossing a line he shouldn't have. He figured they both knew there was no time.

"Come on." Taking her hand, he pulled her to her feet.

"Where are we going?"

"Someplace where the sniper in that chopper can't pick us off."

MATTIE DIDN'T KNOW if she was dizzy from the blow to her head or the kiss that had hit her every bit as hard. But her head was spinning as Cutter took her down the snow-covered trail. She couldn't believe The Jaguar had found them, that they'd come within inches of being blown to smithereens. She couldn't believe hard-nosed Sean Cutter had kissed her senseless. It was the last thing she'd expected him to do. But then, in the last thirty-six hours, she'd come to expect the unexpected.

She could hear the chopper. The roar of the engines. The rotors cutting through the air. The occasional rapid fire of an automatic weapon.

"This way!"

Cutter shouted the words an instant before he went off the trail. The trees they'd been using for cover melted away and they found themselves in a wide, open meadow. The scene might have been beautiful if there hadn't been a madman bent on killing them in hot pursuit. Mattie suddenly felt dangerously exposed. What was Cutter thinking?

"Are you trying to get us killed?" she shouted. "We're sitting ducks here!"

"Trust me."

She tried to wrench her hand free of his, but he tightened his grip and picked up speed. They ran through snow that came up to her knees. The base of some type of steel tower blew past. She was beginning to tire.

A burst of gunfire erupted. A bullet

zinged past her ear. Another ricocheted off an exposed rock. "Cutter, they're shooting at us!"

"Not for long."

He veered left and pulled her into a wild sprint toward a second tower. In the back of her mind it registered that the tower held high-voltage power lines. There was a clearing where crews had cut a swath of trees to build the massive towers. The realization that Cutter was purposefully leading the chopper to the power lines registered just as she heard a thunderous *crack!* Out of the corner of her eye she saw the chopper tilt at a precarious angle. The tail rotor snapped into two pieces. Electricity arced. Sparks flew. White smoke billowed.

An instant later the fuselage exploded. An orange ball rose into the sky like a fiery air balloon. Debris flew outward. The chopper came apart in midair, then huge chunks of twisted steel plummeted to the ground.

"Oh my God," she heard herself say. "They hit the power lines."

Cutter watched the last of the debris hit the ground. "Visibility is poor because of the snow. They couldn't see the wires."

The sight of such utter destruction left her paralyzed. Even though the men in the chopper had been trying to kill them, Mattie suddenly felt an urgent need to help them. "Cutter, we can't just walk away from them."

Without waiting for a response, she extricated her hand from his and started off at a jog toward the downed chopper. "We have to help them."

Cutter caught up with her, captured her arm and spun her to face him. "You don't want to go over there," he said.

"Those men could be...injured or dying."

"Take my word for it, Mattie. There are no survivors."

No survivors.

She knew it was stupid, but the thought of more people dying made her want to cry. "How many people are going to die before this is over?"

Cutter shook his head. "When it comes to The Jaguar, people are expendable." He looked toward the smoldering wreckage. "This proves he will stop at nothing to get the information locked inside your head."

The words made her feel sick. "If he wants me so badly, why don't we just set a trap? Use me as bait?"

Cutter couldn't say he hadn't considered it. He wanted to take down The Jaguar so badly he could taste it. He owed it to himself, owed it to the son of a bitch who'd left his body covered with scars. Martin Wolfe had made it abundantly clear that if it came down to Mattie's life or The Jaguar, she was expendable.

So why haven't you used her as bait, hotshot? a taunting little voice asked.

He didn't like the answer that came to mind. "Because it's my job to take you back."

"You can still accomplish that and use

me as bait." Her expression brightened. "Cutter, The Jaguar is one of the few people who can clear my name. He knows who it was at DOD who gave him the plans for the EDNA project. If he testifies to that—"

"He won't testify."

"Maybe the federal prosecutor will cut him some kind of deal."

"No, Mattie," he snapped.

"But—"

"No. Damn it."

She stared at him, her expression a combination of hurt and anger. She was too eager. Too willing to put herself on the line. The combination gave Cutter a bad feeling in the pit of his stomach. He told himself he was just being conservative, playing it safe. But the truth was he couldn't put her in the line of fire because he cared for her.

"I'm going to see if I can salvage the chopper's radio," he said.

"I'll go with you."

"Stay here," he snapped.

"Cutter, I can help."

"Damn it, Mattie, you don't want to see that wreckage."

He started toward the downed chopper.

"IMBECILES! ALL OF THEM!" The Jaguar snapped the cell phone shut and threw it across the room. The one thing he could not tolerate was incompetence, and he seemed to be surrounded by it.

The two men standing at his desk shifted uncomfortably as they waited for their next orders.

Furious, The Jaguar stared them down. "You were on the radio with them when this accident occurred?"

One of the men nodded. "That's correct."

"How did this happen?"

"One of the men in the chopper had just spotted the scientist on the ground. They followed. Visibility was poor. I can only assume the pilot didn't see the power lines." The man shrugged. "I heard screaming..."

The Jaguar didn't care about the men who'd died. All he cared about was the scientist. And Sean Cutter, the bastard. He knew Cutter was just good enough to have engineered such an accident. Even though he hated the man, he felt a grudging moment of respect for him. "The chopper was equipped with GPS?"

The taller of the two men stepped forward. "We've already got the coordinates."

"Send a team to the wreckage site. I want every available man looking for them."

"We've got two teams en route via snowmobile."

"I want two more teams sent out."

"Done," said the second man.

The two men exchanged looks. "What about the bodies?" one of them asked.

The Jaguar waved off the question. "Leave them. I need every available man searching for that scientist and that bastard agent."

"But, sir—"

"I said leave them!" He strode to a map mounted on the wall. "How far to the nearest town?"

"Six miles. Too far for them to make it on foot in this weather."

He turned to the men. "Don't make the mistake of underestimating Sean Cutter," he said coldly.

"We'll do our best to intercept them before they reach the town."

"The success of our objective depends on the apprehension of that scientist. Rest assured, gentlemen, I will kill the next man who lets them escape. Make sure every man knows that."

"Yes, sir."

"I want them found. I want them brought to me."

And after he extracted the information on the EDNA weapons system, he would take his time killing them both.

Chapter Ten

Cutter found Mattie standing at the base of the nearest tower, her face pale and drawn. Even though she'd wrapped herself in the makeshift poncho, she was shivering. He didn't know if it was from the cold or the shock of seeing the chopper go down, but he was concerned.

"The radio is dead," he said.

Disappointment darkened her lovely features. "Are you sure?"

"It's in pieces." He raised the 9 mm Beretta he'd pilfered from one of the bodies. The pistol was covered with soot but had somehow survived the heat and flames. "This was the only valuable thing I could salvage.

"And the men?"

He shook his head. "No survivors."

She pressed her hand to her stomach. "I'd been hoping…"

The need to comfort her overwhelmed his need for caution. He walked over to her, set his hands on her shoulders and squeezed gently. "Don't think about them," he said.

"I'm not like you," she said. "I can't shut things out."

He wanted to tell her he wasn't so good at it, either, but figured they'd both be better off if he let it go. "We need to keep moving. Find shelter." He looked up at the slate-gray sky. "From the looks of those clouds, there's more snow on the way."

A humorless laugh broke from her lips. "At least there's no one shooting at us."

For now, Cutter thought, and removed the scrap of paper from his pocket. "I found this."

Her eyes flicked down to the paper in his hand. "What is it?"

"Part of a map." He unfolded it, taking care not to damage the burned edges.

"It's pretty scorched. I don't see how it's going to help us."

"Scorched, but not completely destroyed." He set his finger against a circle someone had drawn on the map. "We're here, near the Canadian border."

"Can we get across into Canada?"

"The border is pretty open and wild. As long as we stay off the roads and away from bridges we should be all right."

Her eyes widened as realization set in. "There's a town just a few miles away! We can get to a phone—"

"Six miles to the north, Mattie. It will be a tough hike to say the least. But if we hustle we can make it before dark."

"We can do it."

"We haven't eaten. We don't have gear or clothing."

"Cutter, I can do it." Newfound determination hardened her voice. "I'll do anything to stop this nightmare. I'll do even more to prove I'm innocent."

Staring into her pretty eyes, he didn't have the heart to tell her that she might never get the chance.

MATTIE WAS NO STRANGER to physical exhaustion. In the past forty-eight hours she had become intimately familiar with its every facet. But the trek to Silver Lake, a small ski town in the Canadian province of Alberta, took her beyond exhaustion to a whole new level of misery. Several times, she considered giving up. Just lying down in the snow and letting hypothermia take her to a place where she didn't have to hurt. Only the hope of clearing her name and getting her life back kept her going.

And Sean Cutter.

For the first time since their ordeal had begun, he talked to her. Not as a federal agent, but person to person. He encouraged her. He held her hand when she needed it. He egged her on when all she wanted to do was collapse. He carried her when she finally dropped.

They reached Silver Lake at dusk. It was like stepping into a Bavarian wonderland. Christmas lights adorned ornate streetlamps. Yellow light slanted through the mullioned windows of the storefronts, cafes and shops along the main street.

Mattie took it all in with a weary sense of awe. "I can't believe we made it," she said as they stepped onto the cobblestone sidewalk.

Cutter shot her a smile, touched her shoulder. "You did good, Mattie."

"I want to take a bath. I want to eat a six-course meal and sleep for a week."

"I'll settle for a bed and clean sheets."

"Speaking of." She pointed to a Tudor style bed and breakfast just off the main street.

"Let's hope they have a vacancy," he said.

It did not elude Mattie that Cutter kept

looking over his shoulder or that his eyes continuously scanned the cars moving along the street and the tourists walking the sidewalks. She knew there was a possibility that The Jaguar or some of his men had followed them here. But she was so exhausted, both physically and emotionally, that she didn't have the energy to care.

The clerk greeted them with a halfhearted smile when they entered the bed and breakfast. "Welcome to the Chateau Maurier."

Mattie arched a brow when Cutter spoke to him in fluent French. "What did he say?" she asked.

Cutter grimaced. "They have one room. One bed."

It gave her pause, but only for a moment. "One of us can sleep on the floor."

He turned back to the clerk. "We'll take it."

Cutter paid with cash, and a few minutes later they were opening the door of an A-frame cabin. Once they were inside the first thing Mattie noticed was the warmth. A fire crackled merrily in a beautiful stone hearth. The smell of cloves and sage filled the air. A bowl of ripe fruit sat on the small table. Through the bedroom door, she saw a tall bed piled high with frilly pillows.

"I don't know whether to eat or shower or sleep first," she said.

Cutter smiled, but Mattie sensed an underlying tension she didn't quite understand. Crossing to the table, he picked up two oranges, passed one to her and began to peel the other. "Why don't you take a shower and I'll go round us up something a little more substantial to eat."

"I'll have two of everything," she quipped. "Something rich and French and—" She cut the words short when he just stood there saying nothing. Suddenly it dawned on her that they were not here for relaxation. She was his prisoner. An assignment. He was going to take her back so she could begin her prison sentence. Reality crashed down with all the weight of a boulder.

"Are you going to cuff me to the bed while you're gone?" she asked.

"I was going to tell you to lock the door and not let anyone in."

Uneasiness washed over her. She glanced toward the window. The door. "You think The Jaguar is here?"

"I think he's a determined and ruthless son of a bitch. It's only a matter of time before he finds us."

Mattie knew Cutter wasn't going to sit around and let that happen. He didn't say the words, but she knew he had to call his superiors at whatever agency he worked for. He was going to tell them he had her in custody. Then they were going to come for her.

"I'll be back in a few minutes." He gave her a hard look as he opened the door. "Lock the door behind me and don't let anyone in."

Mattie watched him disappear into the

night, then closed the door and set the dead bolt. She should have been relieved to be safe and warm and alive. But there was a knot in her gut the size of Montana. She wasn't sure when it had happened, but at some point in the past two days Sean Cutter had become more friend than persecutor. It hurt to know he was going to turn her over to the authorities. Mattie wasn't sure what she'd been hoping for, but it wasn't that.

Attributing her melancholy mood to exhaustion, she headed toward the bathroom, shed the poncho and flipped on the light. The image of herself in the mirror caused her to gasp. Her clothes were torn and dirty. Soot streaked her face. Her hair looked as if some big bird had nested in it. She couldn't help it; she laughed out loud. It was either that or cry.

She turned on the shower, stepped beneath the spray and let the hot water beat down on her. Putting her face in her hands, she sobbed and tried desperately not to think about spending the rest of her life in prison.

CUTTER PICKED UP clothes at a local boutique and two cell phones at a small electronics store. He found a sandwich shop one block over and stopped in for sandwiches and soft drinks.

On his way back he kept an eye on the streets and sidewalks, but no one seemed unduly interested in him. To make sure he wasn't followed, he circled the block twice and cut through an alley before heading to the bed and breakfast.

He unlocked the door and was immediately aware of the sound of the shower. As he set the food on the table, he tried hard not to think about Mattie, but his efforts were in vain. In his mind's eye he saw water sluicing over milky flesh. He saw soap bubbles clinging to secret curves. He saw her head thrown back in ecstasy as he drove into her…

"Smells wonderful."

Cutter *never* blushed. But standing there, semierect and indulging in thoughts he had no business indulging in, heat crept into his cheeks.

"Are you all right?" Concern darkened her eyes as she crossed the room to him.

The fluffy white robe was two sizes too big, but at that moment Cutter thought he'd never seen a more beautiful woman. Her wet hair was slicked back, revealing her high cheekbones and porcelain skin. Her brows were thin and very dark, off-setting her big, pretty eyes. Her hands were red and chapped from the cold, but her bones were fine. Even her feet were sexy.

"I'm fine," he growled, but he broke a sweat beneath his flannel shirt.

Before he could turn away, she reached out and pressed her fingertips to his forehead. "My God," she said, "You're perspiring. I think you may have a fever."

He had a fever all right. But the heat

running through his veins had nothing to do with being sick. "I'm going to take a shower."

Turning away from her, he started for the bathroom.

"Cutter?"

He stopped, but didn't face her. "What is it?"

"We haven't talked about what's going to happen next."

He felt a hard tug of regret. He knew all too well what he had to do. What he had been putting off. He had to contact Martin Wolfe and tell him he had Mattie Logan in custody. Within hours two agents would arrive to transport her to prison. Hell, he should have contacted Martin Wolfe the instant he arrived in town. He should have her cuffed and shackled for when the agents arrived to transport her to prison…

Instead he was sharing a meal with her and fantasizing about all the things he wanted to do to her….

"I'm dead on my feet," he said. "We'll talk after I get cleaned up. After we eat."

Not wanting to see the hurt on her face, he turned and started for the shower.

CUTTER FELT ALMOST HUMAN after he'd washed off the grime and cold. His ribs were severely bruised, but none of the wounds appeared to be infected. Wrapping himself in a navy-blue robe, he left the bathroom. Mattie had set out the sandwiches and cut up several pieces of fruit. She was sitting at the table with her face in her hands looking bone weary.

"You didn't have to wait for me," he said. "You could have eaten."

"My parents raised me to have good manners." She shot him a smile that was more sad than wry. "But then, I don't think anyone cares about good manners in prison, do they?"

Cutter didn't know what to say. He sank into a chair and reached for his sandwich. "Eat," he said.

Neither of them spoke as they delved

into their food. But it wasn't a comfortable silence. There was a tension between them that hadn't been there before.

"Cutter, after everything we've been through, the least you can do is tell me what's going to happen next," she said after a moment.

"I've got to check in. File a report."

"And then?"

"Our being in Canada will complicate things a little, but the agency has a lot of pull when it comes to cutting through jurisdictional red tape." He sighed. "Once that's taken care of, a couple of U.S. Marshals will pick you up here and you'll be transported to a secure location. You'll be asked to give a statement that will go on record. From there you'll be taken to a federal prison."

"I didn't do it," she whispered. "I don't want to go to prison."

"Mattie, I told you I'd look into your case."

"Daniel Savage is a smart man. He was

careful. My defense attorney was good. She and her army of investigators couldn't find anything to save me. What makes you think you can?"

"I'm better."

"You're not going to risk your career for the likes of me. You don't know me. You don't care about—"

"I care," he said.

"If you cared you would not turn me in."

"It's not that simple."

"It is if you want it to be."

Cutter set down his sandwich and gave her a hard look. "Doing the right thing and doing what I want are not one and the same."

"What is it you want, Cutter?" Throwing down her napkin, she rose abruptly. "Justice? The truth?"

"I'm trying to do the right thing."

"Yeah? Well here's a newsflash for you— you're not. I'm innocent and you're doing your utmost to send me to prison. What can possibly be right about that?"

"I can't bend the rules because they don't suit you," he said. "Damn it, I have to go about this the right way. There's protocol. I'll need proof before I can help you."

"Don't tell me about protocol or proof or right and wrong. My life is destroyed. If you take me back none of that is going to save me."

Angry now, Cutter flung down his napkin and surged to his feet. "A little trust on your part would go a long way right now."

"Trusting the wrong person is how I got into this mess in the first place," she returned.

"I'm nothing like Savage," he said.

"No, you're just a little more up-front about wanting to ruin my life."

"Damn it, Mattie, I care."

"Care about what?" she said. "Protocol?"

He looked into her eyes. "You," he said, and started toward her.

Chapter Eleven

Mattie stared at Cutter. The draw she felt to him was like a powerful magnet, pulling her with undeniable force.

"It's the truth." Cutter stopped a scant foot away from her. So close she could smell the soap from his shower. "You don't spend two days with someone fighting for your life and not know what they're made of."

"Thank you for saying that," she said after a moment.

"Try to be patient," he said. "Trust me. Can you do that?"

She studied him for a long time. Such

a hardened face. But his eyes did not lie. "Okay."

"Sit back down and eat."

Feeling more relaxed, she returned to her chair and sat. But her mind was spinning. Did he truly care about her? Or would he forget about her once she was locked away.

Trust me.

Oh, how she wanted to put her trust in him. But Mattie had been badly burned by Daniel Savage. She knew Cutter was nothing like him. Still, the one thing the two men did share was an agenda. Cutter's was to take her in.

It was the one thing she could not allow.

They ate without speaking. When Mattie finished, she rose and walked to the window and looked out at the snowy landscape beyond. She chose her next words carefully. "The Jaguar can clear me, Cutter."

"We have to catch him first."

"I agree." She turned, watched his eyes narrow. "The best, maybe the only way to catch him is staring you right in the face. For some reason you're not seeing it."

"Don't go there, Mattie."

"Use me as bait."

"No," he said flatly.

"You know it will work."

"I know it's a bad idea."

"Bad for whom?"

"For you."

"That's where you're wrong. Don't you see? All of us win. You get your man. I get cleared. And we nab this bastard once and for all."

His jaw flexed. "If he gets his hands on you, he'll kill you."

"It's a risk I'm willing to take."

"I'm not."

"It's my decision."

"The hell it is," he said. "Damn it, Mattie, you have no idea what that son of a bitch is capable of."

"I think I do."

A rough sound that was supposed to be

a laugh ground from his throat. "You don't have a clue."

"I know that I'd rather face death than life in prison for something I didn't do!"

Cutter jumped to his feet. When Mattie turned away, he grabbed her arm, and with his other hand he ripped open his shirt. Buttons flew and bounced on the floor. He worked the shirt from his body and flung it onto the back of a chair. Then he turned his back to her.

She gasped at the sight of the angry red scars crisscrossing his back. It was as if his flesh had been melted, removed and then dribbled back on like hot wax. It struck her that even when she'd treated his bullet wound, he'd never allowed her to see his back. Now she knew why, and her heart shattered.

"My God," she heard herself say. "Cutter…"

"This is what he's capable of," he said in a low voice. "Take a good long look before you decide you want to use yourself as bait."

Mattie put her hand over her mouth in shock. She knew the physical wounds on this man's back had long since healed. But how could someone ever recover from such a terrible ordeal? Cutter had suffered agonies she couldn't imagine. What kind of monster could do something like this? The knowledge that this had been intentionally done by another human being outraged her, sickened her.

"The Jaguar did that to you?" she asked.

"Took him fourteen hours, but he got the job done." Cutter turned to her, his face an unreadable mask. "Take my word for it. You don't want to cross him."

Her mind was reeling. She'd always suspected there was something personal between Cutter and The Jaguar. Now she knew what that something was, and it horrified her. "I'm sorry," she heard herself say.

"Don't be." Bending he snatched his shirt from the floor. "Those scars keep me focused. They help me do my job."

She didn't know what to say. She remembered the nightmare he'd wakened from and wondered what agonies were locked inside his head.

He started to put on the shirt. Before Mattie realized she was going to move she was out of the chair and going to him. She didn't know what she was going to do once she reached him. All she knew was that this man had suffered horribly. The need to take away his pain, to give him what little comfort she could superceded the need for caution, the need to protect herself.

He jolted when she put her hand on his shoulder. Surprise and caution and another emotion she couldn't quite read filled his eyes when he turned to her.

"He hurt you," she said.

"I screwed up. The Jaguar upheld his reputation."

"Cutter, he's a monster."

"My point exactly." He made another attempt to pull on the shirt. When she stopped him, he shot her a questioning look. "Mattie…"

"You don't have to hide them from me."

"They're…grotesque."

"They're not," she whispered. "They're part of you."

"A part of me you don't want to know."

"Maybe I do. Maybe I want to know all of you."

His gaze searched hers with an intensity that had her heart racing. "We both know this can't go anywhere."

She could see the rapid rise and fall of his chest. Caution flickered in his eyes when she raised her hand and touched his cheek.

"Don't," he said, but the word was little more than a puff of breath on his lips.

"Why?"

"Because I'm not a strong enough man to stop you."

"Or maybe deep inside you know I'm not what they say I am," she said, and raised her mouth to his.

CUTTER HAD KNOWN this moment would come. He'd known it was inevitable. As a federal agent he knew he should resist. But as a man, powerfully attracted to her, he suddenly didn't care about right or wrong or repercussions.

He didn't kiss her back. His body went rigid on contact. He went so far as to set his hands on her slender shoulders, but he didn't push her away. Instead, his fingers dug into the softness of her shoulders. Growling low in his throat, he pulled her against him.

Her mouth was wet and soft against his. Her body conformed to his with utter perfection. He was aware of her arms going around his shoulders, her body going liquid against his. He'd wanted to kiss her for so long, and he reveled in the sheer pleasure of it.

He assured himself he would come to his senses in a moment. He knew better than to get caught up in a moment like this. Two years ago he'd fallen prey to temptation while in the midst of a mission, and he'd nearly paid with his life. He'd sworn never to do it again.

But sanity refused to rally. When she sighed and snuggled closer, he knew he had to have more.

He deepened the kiss. She opened to him. His tongue entwined with hers. In the back of his mind a sane little voice cried out for him to pull away and regroup. But the need to feel her body against his was consuming.

Blood rushed hotly to his groin. She was small and soft and curvy. A groan of pleasure escaped him when she put her hands against his chest. He shuddered when her fingertips skimmed over his nipples. The floor tilted beneath his feet when she wrapped her fingers around him.

Cutter knew he was about to cross a

line. He knew it was a line that couldn't be traversed a second time. This transgression could cost him his career. But with her mouth against his and the knowledge that she was innocent pounding through him in perfect time with his heart, he could no more stop what they were about to do than he could stop breathing.

He swept her into his arms and started for the bed.

THERE WERE A THOUSAND reasons why Mattie should not be kissing Sean Cutter. First and foremost there was the matter of his being a federal agent and her status as his prisoner. That hard cold fact stood squarely in the way of anything ever coming of this moment.

But the sensation of his mouth against hers was like a drug, making her do things she normally wouldn't do. She realized she was making a mistake. The knowledge that it wasn't the first one rapped at her brain like insistent knuckles against a door. Mattie had made a terrible mistake by trusting the wrong person once before. She'd given her heart to Daniel Savage only to have him betray her. Could she be making the same mistake again?

But Cutter was nothing like Savage. His character rose far above that of her former coworker. He was a straight shooter. But he was still a man. They had spent over thirty-six intense, high-adrenaline hours together. Had the intensity of the situation brought about this moment? Or were the emotions, the sensations coursing through her coming from someplace deeper?

He reached the bed, let her slide to her feet and kissed her hard on the mouth. His fingertips were electric against her skin, and she felt the tingle all the way to her bones, the pleasure drowning out the nagging doubts and questions plaguing her mind.

His palms were warm and slightly

rough against her face. "You know this is risky business," he said roughly.

"I know," she said. "Your job…"

"Risky for both of us," he cut in. "Not just me."

Confusion swirled for an instant. "You mean it doesn't change anything."

"It changes everything," he corrected. "But I still have to do my job."

"Cutter, you know I'm innocent."

"I know."

Emotion formed a knot in her throat, but she swallowed it. "You said you'd help me."

"I will, Mattie. I promise, I'll do my best to clear your name." His jaw tightened. "But I still have to take you in. If I don't, we both become fugitives and that will only make everything worse."

Hurt twisted inside her. She'd known he was the kind of man who would do his job no matter what. She just hadn't expected it to hurt so badly. "Cutter, I can help you bring down The Jaguar."

"No," he growled.

"Please," she said, "I'll do anything to stay out of prison."

"I'm not going to let you put yourself in danger."

"It's my choice, Cutter. Not yours. Don't take what little hope I have left away from me."

"Mattie," he snapped. "I've seen his file. The Jaguar has a classic sociopath profile. He doesn't hurt people because he has to. He does it because he *enjoys* it."

She thought of the horrendous scars on his back, and tears burned her eyes. "Don't you see? That's all the more reason to stop him."

"Listen to me, Mattie. I'll do everything in my power to clear your name. But I have to take you back first. I know it's hard, but you're going to have to trust me on this."

She hadn't realized her tears had spilled over until he raised his hand and wiped a tear from her cheek with his thumb. She raised her gaze to his. She knew he was going to kiss her. She should stop him; she knew he would ultimately hurt her. But she simply wasn't strong enough.

The kiss devastated her. A sob caught in her throat, but he smothered it with a second kiss so powerful it took her breath. She could feel her body responding to his. The hurt and pleasure mingling into a bittersweet pool around her heart.

When he untied the robe and tugged it open, she shuddered. "Aw, man, you're beautiful," he whispered.

She started to say something, but he brushed his fingertips against her sensitized nipples. The sensation stole her voice, made her knees weak, her head spin. She sank onto the bed. He came down on top of her. Capturing her mouth with his, he gently worked the robe from her body. His skin seemed to sizzle against hers. She could feel the hard length of his shaft against her belly. She heard his quickened breaths. She felt the urgency of his touch. Felt that same urgency zinging through her blood.

She opened to him. A groan rumbled up from his chest when he slid into her and went deep. Every muscle in his body went taut. He whispered her name. Once. Twice. When he began to move, she moved with him, taking him deep and then rising up to meet him. Pleasure warred with the pain of knowing this might be their one and only time together. And even as the ecstasy rose to a fever pitch, her heart shattered into a thousand pieces.

Chapter Twelve

Cutter was not an impulsive man. He liked to think a situation or problem through before acting. He always erred on the side of caution. When it came to women he was wary. He could count the number of women he'd been intimate with on one hand. Sleeping with a prisoner he'd been hired to apprehend and transport was the most irresponsible, reckless thing he'd ever done. Not only with regard to his career, but on a personal level, as well.

How are you going to turn her over to the Department of Corrections now, hotshot?

The question taunted him as he lay in the darkness and listened to her steady breathing. The memory of their lovemaking still resonated through his body, through his heart. Cutter was not a sentimental man, but somehow Mattie Logan to managed to touch him in a place he guarded well.

"Even in the darkness I can see that you're troubled."

He glanced over at her. She'd propped herself up on one elbow. Even though she held the sheet at her breast to cover herself, the sight of her took his breath away. It was going to kill him to take her back.

Leaning back in the pillows, he patted the area next to him and beckoned her to snuggle. "I wish there was another way to do this."

She curled beside him, like a cat taking a sunbath. Her skin was warm and silky against his. Cutter closed his eyes against the quick swipe of pleasure, the hard tug of lust.

"There is," she said. "We could go on the offensive."

"Don't go there."

Cutter stared at the ceiling and brooded. He was starting to think she'd fallen asleep when she spoke.

"What happened between you and The Jaguar?"

He didn't want to talk about it. The memory was a dark place he never ventured. But he knew if he was going to succeed in deterring her, it was something he was going to have to share. "It's ugly," he said.

"I know," she said simply. "I've seen the scars."

Cutter pondered where to start. So much had happened on that mission.

"I was an operative with the CIA for twelve years," he began. "I worked deep undercover. First in South America during the drug war. After 9/11, I focused on infiltrating terrorist cells. I was good at it."

"What happened?"

"A little over two years ago I was sent to Paris to infiltrate a cell. The CIA had created a new identity for me. We knew this cell was planning something big. We knew it was run by a man known only as The Jaguar. I was to report back to the CIA what they were planning."

"That must have been harrowing work."

He smiled, but it felt tight on his face. "I was into the adrenaline of it back then. There was no assignment too dangerous. I knew how to handle myself, think fast on my feet. I had that nine-lives thing going."

"What went wrong?"

"The French government was also working to infiltrate this cell. They sent in a female operative. Her name was Monique. It took months of hard work to get close to this group. Months of isolation. Being surrounded by radicals and murderers. Pretending to be one of them. Knowing Monique was one of the good guys helped get me through it. We became friends." He grimaced. "We became more than friends."

"You were lovers?"

He nodded. "It was unprofessional. Reckless. I knew it, but by then I was so burned out I couldn't stop seeing her. She was the only light in my life. I saw things during those months…" Remembering, he let his voice trail. "This group was brutal. Fanatical. Dangerous as hell. I knew they were planning something big. Once I figured out what that something was, I could get out. But until I had the goods, I had to hold on. Monique helped me do that." Bitterness rose inside him. "Or so I thought."

"What happened?"

"By then I was living in North Africa, sleeping in an underground bunker with about twelve other men, all of them terrorists. I'd been inside for about eight months when it happened." Sweat broke out on his skin and he threw the covers from his chest. "Six armed men stormed the bunker in the wee hours. They woke me up. The Jaguar was there. One look, and I knew my cover had been blown."

"That must have been terrifying."

"I did my best to convince them otherwise. I simply couldn't figure out how they'd made me. The CIA had been meticulous. I'd been careful." He blew out a sigh. "Well, I'd been careful in every area except for one."

"Monique," Mattie guessed.

Cutter nodded and tried not to feel like a fool. "They took me to an old prison, part of which was underground. The room was windowless. There were restraints. Electricity. Instruments of torture. I knew what was going to happen. The Jaguar was in charge, and I knew he was going to try to make me talk. Either that or kill me trying."

THE HORROR HE MUST HAVE FELT knowing that he was going to be tortured, probably to death. "Oh Cutter."

"It never entered my mind that Monique was the one who'd given me up until I saw her there. In that terrible room. At first I thought they had found her out, too. That she would be tortured. Then I realized she was a double agent for The Jaguar—and his lover, as well. The Jaguar has a reputation for being wildly jealous. He knew I'd slept with Monique. And he took great pleasure in having me at his mercy."

Mattie couldn't speak. She hurt for him. Snuggling closer, she set her hand against his chest, where his heart pounded out of control.

"I spent fourteen hours in that room with that son of a bitch."

Tears burned her eyes. She could feel the sweat slicking his skin. The hammering of his heart. The tremors ripping through his body. To see such a strong man in the throes of a panic attack broke her heart. She wanted to stop the memories from torturing him, but didn't know how. The best she could do was hold him and hope he could take comfort in her closeness.

"I'm sorry you had to go through that," she said.

"I won't lie to you, Mattie. It was…bad. Those hours were like death. They were worse than death. In the end I prayed for death." He looked away, gathered himself, then met her gaze. "That's why I don't want you anywhere near The Jaguar."

"Cutter, he needs to be stopped. He's a maniac—"

"I'll get him."

"And let this opportunity slip by?"

His lips tightened, but he said nothing.

"I'm your ace in the hole." Mattie tapped her finger against her temple. "He wants what I have in my head. The next phase for the EDNA Project. You put me on a hook and he's going to bite."

"And take a piece of you."

"Not if we don't let him."

"Two years ago I thought I had a safety

net. I thought the agency would look out for me. Well, guess what, Mattie? They didn't get there in time."

"I know you can keep me safe."

"When it comes to The Jaguar, safety is an illusion."

"You'd rather I go to prison?"

"Until I can find what I need to exonerate you."

"What if you don't find it, Cutter?"

"Look, I'm not saying this is going to be easy."

"I'm not willing to risk spending the rest of my life in jail for something I didn't do!"

"And I'm not willing to risk turning you over to a monster who will extract the information he needs and then torture you to death!" he said brutally. "He'll do it, Mattie. Not only because he enjoys it, but because he knows it will be a way to get back at me for sleeping with Monique."

He stared at her, his eyes furious and

intense. For the first time Mattie realized he was not simply afraid. He was terrified. Not for himself, but for her. Unable to keep herself from it, she reached for him.

"I'm afraid, too, Cutter."

"Then listen to me. Trust me on this."

"I don't know what to do."

He pulled her against him, held her tight. "Let me keep you safe."

But when he pulled her closer, the dynamics of the situation changed. Mattie knew the moment was about to spiral out of control. There was too much intensity. Too many emotions. All of it about to explode. Before she could draw away, his mouth found hers. He tasted of desperation and fear. She returned his kiss, letting her own emotions take control.

He made love to her like there was no tomorrow. For Mattie there wasn't. All they had was this small, precious moment in time. She knew it was fleeting. She reveled in it, clung to it.

Because first chance she got she was going to walk away and stop The Jaguar herself.

Chapter Thirteen

Cutter waited until she was asleep before rising. He shut the bedroom door and went into the living room. With a heavy heart he picked up the phone.

Martin Wolfe answered on the first ring. "Where the hell are you?"

"In a safe place."

"Do you have Mattie Logan?"

"I've got her."

"Where are you? I'll have a couple of agents pick her up."

Cutter hesitated. "Martin, something isn't right about this case."

"What are you talking about?" Wolfe asked cautiously.

"I'm talking about Mattie Logan."

"What about her?"

"I think someone else may be involved."

"Cutter, you're making me very uneasy."

"She didn't do it."

Wolfe made a rude sound. "Stop right there."

"The person who sold the EDNA plans to The Jaguar is still out there."

"And you know this how?"

Cutter knew what the other man would think. Hating it that he would be partially right. "We were holed up for a couple a days under difficult circumstances. The information she gave me is credible."

"You believe her."

"Yes."

A sigh hissed over the line. "Tell me you did not cross a line with her."

Now it was Cutter's turn to remain silent.

"Oh, for God's sake! You slept with her?"

Another long, uncomfortable silence.

Wolfe cursed. "You were the one operative I figured I could count on to do this right!"

"I brought her in."

"What you brought in is a potential lawsuit against the agency. For God's sake, Sean, she could make all sorts of claims against you. It could affect a case that took federal prosecutors months to put together."

"She won't."

Wolfe laughed, but it was a cynical sound. "The shrink warned me you weren't ready to go back into the field. I should have listened."

"She didn't do it, Martin. I'm going to prove it."

"Let the judicial system take care of Logan. I want you to concentrate on bringing in The Jaguar. This is the closest we've been to him since…"

"Since he nearly tortured me to death," Cutter finished brutally.

"He needs to be stopped."

"I'll get him."

"You could use Logan to smoke him out."

"No."

"That bastard needs her. He's not going to kill her."

"I'm not going to put a civilian in that kind of danger."

"She put herself in danger."

Cutter scrubbed a hand over his jaw, aware that he hadn't shaved for two days. "I'll think of something else," he said.

"She's your best bet and you know it," Wolfe said.

"She's been through enough."

Wolfe swore. "Where are you?"

Knowing if he wanted to keep Mattie safe, he didn't have a choice but to send her back, Cutter closed his eyes, hating what he had to do. "I'm at the Chateau Maurier in Silver Lake. In Alberta."

"I can have two U.S. Marshalls there in a couple of hours."

"What about jurisdiction?"

"You know I can take care of any jurisdiction or extradition problem with one phone call." Wolfe paused. "Two hours, Sean."

"I'll be here," Cutter said and disconnected.

MATTIE STOOD at the bedroom door and listened as Cutter gave the man on the other end of the phone line their location. She couldn't believe he was going to turn her over to the authorities after everything they'd been through. Was he doing it because he cared for her and wanted to keep her safe as he claimed? Or had she been a fool and let him use her in the worse possible way a man could use a woman?

The questions hit her like a punch to the stomach. She nearly doubled over with the pain. She didn't know what to think. Sean Cutter seemed like a straight shooter. But six months ago, so had Daniel Savage. The one thing she did know for certain was that she was not going to prison.

She took a final look at Cutter. He'd hung up the phone and was sitting on the sofa with his elbows on his knees, his face in his hands. He looked...broken. The need to go to him was great. But Mattie couldn't let herself. No matter how painful—no matter how dangerous—she had to do this.

Quietly she eased the door shut and backed away from it. Looking around quickly, she gathered the clothes Cutter had bought for her when he'd picked up their dinner. She slipped into the parka and spotted one of two cell phones he'd bought lying on the night table. She snatched it up and dropped it into her pocket. Never taking her eyes from the sliver of light beneath the door, praying he didn't walk in before she could get out, she crept to the window. The wooden sill creaked when she opened it.

Squeezing her body through the opening, she slid outside into the frigid night air and set off at a run.

CUTTER FELT LIKE HELL. Truth be told, he felt worse than hell. He felt as if he'd betrayed Mattie. That he'd made love to her just minutes before turning her in gave the situation a cruel twist.

After hanging up the phone, he sat on the sofa trying to come up with a way out of this mess. But all he could think of was Mattie. The way she'd looked at him when he touched her cheek. The heat in her eyes when he kissed her. The way her eyes had glazed in pleasure when he'd been inside her.

Martin Wolfe was right. He'd crossed a line with her. Put a black mark on his career. But the worst thing he'd done was betray a woman he cared for deeply. *Too deeply,* he thought.

The realization that he'd fallen for her frightened him. Cutter was a whiz at dodging bullets, but to be confronted with feelings so overwhelming was something else altogether—and a hell of a lot more terrifying.

Cursing, he rose. He looked at the bedroom door where she lay sleeping just beyond. The need to go to her and spend these last hours with her ate at him like acid. But he knew making love to her again after what he'd done would only make things worse. It would only make their inevitable parting more painful for both of them.

Better for him to get some sleep. He was mentally and physically exhausted. He needed distance from her. From all the things she made him feel. From the emotions boiling inside him.

He went to the closet in the bathroom and pulled out a pillow and blanket. Carrying them back to the sofa, he flipped off the light. But as he lay down in the darkness and stared at the ceiling, he knew sleep would not come.

MATTIE SAT in a booth of the coffee shop, looking past the cup of cold coffee in front of her. Outside fluffy snowflakes floated down from the night sky. It was a beautiful scene, and she wished she could have shared it with Cutter.

She wondered if he'd discovered that she was missing. If federal agents were on their way to pick her up. She didn't have much time.

Judging from the conversation she'd overheard, Cutter's superior wanted to use her as bait. That she had been right was little consolation. Evidently, the agency he worked for had deemed her expendable.

Over coffee she formulated a plan. A plan that was dangerous at best. Deadly at worst. The prospect of facing The Jaguar terrified her. But if she wanted her life back, she was going to have to do this.

Picking up the cell phone, she checked the outgoing calls. One call to a Washington, D.C., area code had been made. She could only assume Cutter had called his superior. Praying she got the right person, she hit the redial button and waited.

"Martin Wolfe," came a curt male voice on the other end of the line.

"This is Mattie Logan," she said.

The silence lasted so long that she thought they'd been disconnected. "Are you still there?" she asked.

"Where's Cutter? And what are you doing with his cell phone?"

"He's fine." She took a deep breath and plunged. "I want to help you catch The Jaguar."

Another long silence. "Put Cutter on the phone."

"The Jaguar wants something I have. I want to help you catch him."

"I don't deal with—"

"Cutter won't use me because he…he doesn't want to put me in danger. I don't think you have any such qualms, do you, Mr. Wolfe?"

"Put Cutter on the phone. Now."

"I can help you capture The Jaguar. You know I can. Damn it, let me do this."

"Why?"

"Because I'm innocent and I'll do anything to stay out of prison."

A brief hesitation. "Keep talking."

"Daniel Savage was my coworker at the Department of Defense. Over a period of several months he stole confidential information from me and sold it to The Jaguar. Then he proceeded to frame me."

"Savage was cleared."

"Someone didn't look closely enough at the evidence."

Wolfe said nothing.

Mattie played her ace. "He's going to sell the next phase of EDNA if someone doesn't stop him."

"What's your plan?"

"I call Savage and ask for his help. Tell him I need money and ask him to wire it. I'll wait for it at the telegraph office here in Silver Lake. Chances are, The Jaguar or one of his men will show."

"You expect me to trust you?"

"If you want The Jaguar, you don't have a choice."

"How is your plan going to help me take down The Jaguar?"

"When The Jaguar shows up at the wire office for me," she continued, "your men can nab him."

"How do you know The Jaguar won't send one of his thugs?"

"Because I think this has become personal for him. There's something between him and Cutter."

"He told you about what happened in Africa?"

"Yes."

"And you're not afraid?"

"I'm terrified." A sigh shuddered out of her. "But I want my life back. I'm willing to do this."

"How do I know you're not going to take the first bus out of there?"

"Because you trust Sean Cutter's instincts."

He sighed heavily. "Where is he?"

"At the chateau. He doesn't know I'm gone."

The man on the other end of the line swore softly. "Well, he's in for a surprise, isn't he?"

Mattie regretted doing that to him. He'd trusted her. But she had to believe that in the long run it would be worth it.

"Call me with the time and location," Wolfe said. "I've got agents en route. They should be there in a couple of hours."

"Okay."

"If you run when this is through, I'll throw every resource I have at catching you."

"I'm not going to run," she said. "But I want your word that when this is over I can count on you to do the right thing."

The silence that followed was thoughtful. "I'll have someone take a closer look at Savage."

"And the evidence he used to frame me."

"All right. I'll see what I can do."

For now Mattie had to settle for the faint hope he offered by that. What other choice did she have?

Chapter Fourteen

Cutter woke suddenly and with a bad feeling. For the first night in months he hadn't dreamed of The Jaguar or the fourteen hours he'd spent in agonizing pain. Instead he'd dreamed it had been Mattie strapped to that gurney and at the mercy of a madman....

He sat up abruptly, his heart pounding, his body slicked with sweat. The room felt empty. It was too quiet. Mattie had a way of filling up a room just with her presence. He knew she was gone even before he crossed to the bedroom door and opened it.

She'd gone to the trouble of placing the

two pillows beneath the comforter to make it look as if she were in the bed. But the window was ajar, the drapes rippling as the icy wind blasted inside.

An emotion filled curse broke from his lips. It was not the sound of an agent who'd lost his prisoner, but the sound of a man who feared for the life of the woman he loved.

Loved.

Where the hell had that come from?

The question flitted through his mind as he rushed to the living room and quickly put on his clothes. Cutter tried to think rationally. Where had she gone? He knew she wouldn't have run merely to escape. Her mind didn't work that way.

Then suddenly the truth dawned on him. She was going after The Jaguar.

Sick with dread, he sat down hard on the bed. In the past he'd always been good at keeping his emotions out of his work. But knowing that Mattie was out there alone and willing to put herself on the line shook him to his core. It was foolhardy. Suicidal, if he wanted to be honest about it. But Mattie was smart. She knew she possessed the one thing The Jaguar wanted most, the single most powerful tool with which to draw him in: the future plans for the EDNA Project. But how was she going to handle the situation once she found herself face-to-face with a madman?

Mattie was eons out of her league. She was desperate and willing to risk every-thing—including her life—to clear her name. She thought the knowledge locked inside her head would protect her. But Cutter knew otherwise. Once The Jaguar extracted the information he needed, he would kill her.

Fear sent him to his feet. He had to find her and fast. Before she did something crazy. Something irrevocable. Because once The Jaguar got his hands on her, Cutter feared he would never see her again.

Snagging his coat from the sofa, he headed for the door.

MATTIE DIALED Daniel Savage's number from memory and waited, her hands trembling. He answered on the second ring.

"Daniel?"

"Mattie?" Shock laced his voice. "My God. I was watching the news and heard about your escape."

"I didn't escape, but I don't have time to go into that right now."

"Are you all right? Are you hurt?"

"I'm okay. But I need your help."

"You know I'll do anything to help you. Anything at all."

She felt a wave of anger, but quickly shoved her emotions aside. "I need some money."

"All right. How much? I'll send you whatever you need. Just tell me where you are."

A quiver of uncertainty went through her. Once she revealed her location to him, her plan would be set into motion and there would be nothing she could do to stop it. If Daniel was the one who'd framed her—and she was certain he was—he would contact The Jaguar. The Jaguar would come for her. Could she handle the terrorist on her own?

"I'm in Alberta," she said. "A ski resort near the U.S. border called Silver Lake."

"Is there a wire office?"

"Yes." She rattled off the phone number of the tiny shop on the edge of town, next to the post office. "Five hundred dollars should tide me over."

"Tide you over until what, Mattie? My God, the police are looking for you. What are you hoping to accomplish?"

"I think someone framed me, Daniel."

A beat of silence. "Who?"

"I don't know. But I'm going to find out."

"Honey, maybe you should let the authorities handle it."

She cringed at the endearment. "I'm not going to prison."

"I'll wire the money immediately."

"I'm using an alias." She mind spun through several names. "Donna Clark."

"You got it."

"Thank you, Daniel." She looked through the window at the wire office across the street. "I'll be waiting."

"Take care of yourself," he said.

"SILVER LAKE?"

"That's what we were told."

The Jaguar looked at the map pinned to the wall and pondered how to best handle the situation. "That's an hour from here."

"She'll be waiting at the wire office for the money to be sent."

"Excellent." He looked at his watch. "Is there an airport?"

"Yes. It's a ski resort. Lots of small planes flying in and out."

"Have my jet fueled and ready to go in ten minutes."

"Yes, sir."

"And be sure to reward our contact in

Washington, D.C., for his loyalty. Ten thousand dollars ought to keep him happy."

"I'll make sure he gets the money."

"Good. We will continue to treat him well as long as he remains useful."

"I'll meet you at the landing strip in ten minutes."

The Jaguar disconnected and walked to his desk. He smiled as he opened the manila folder containing the file he'd compiled on Mattie Logan. Her photograph smiled up at him. *So lovely*, he thought. *It would be a shame to mar that face.* He wondered how long it would take to make her talk.

Anticipation zinged through him. He would finally have the plans for EDNA. He would finally have the power he needed to bring the West to its knees.

Then he would have the pleasure of killing Mattie Logan.

THE TOWN OF SILVER LAKE was small, but one man could only cover so much ground. Cutter started on the west end of town and worked his way east. He stopped at every business—the café, the boutique, the antique store, even the bookstore, and asked about the young woman with big blue eyes. But no one had seen her. Where the hell had she gone?

Before leaving the bed and breakfast he'd discovered she'd taken one of the cell phones. He'd called the number a dozen times, but she hadn't picked up. Damn her. Didn't she realize what this was doing to him? After twenty minutes of striking out, he was nearly out of his mind with worry. Had The Jaguar already found her? Had she become frightened and gone on the run? Either way, she was in terrible danger. He had to find her. But how?

Cutter hadn't wanted to enlist the help of the agency. Not because he was trying to save face; he'd long since concerned himself with anything so superficial. But

Mattie's life was on the line. It was only smart to use every available resource to find her.

Pulling the cell phone from his pocket, he called Martin Wolfe. "She's gone," he said simply when the other man picked up.

"I know," the other man said.

It wasn't the response Cutter had been expecting. His stomach twisted into a knot. "What the hell are you talking about?"

"She called me, Sean."

The words crashed over him like a tidal wave. "You had better start talking."

"I figured she would have called you by now."

Cutter's heart began to pound. "She didn't. So, talk to me, damn it."

"She's going to try to make contact with The Jaguar. Use herself as bait. Try to set him up so we can move in."

He swore darkly. "Tell me you did not go along with it."

"You know as well as I do that she's our

best bet for nabbing that sick son of a bitch. If you weren't personally involved with her you'd see that as clearly as I do."

Uh-oh, Cutter thought. Of all the things he'd anticipated Mattie doing, calling his superior was not one of them. He sure as hell hadn't expected a man of Wolfe's professional stature to go along with her cockamamie scheme.

"When were you going to clue me in on this?" Cutter snarled.

"She was supposed to call you."

"Since when you do rely on a civilian to keep me informed?"

"Since you lost control of the situation."

Cutter wanted to reach through the phone line and strangle the other man but knew he didn't have a leg to stand on. He wasn't exactly sure when it had happened, but he *had* lost control of the situation. As hard as he'd tried to combat his feelings for Mattie, he admitted he was running on emotions now, not logic. If he could just put his feelings for her aside, he might be able to think through this and get to her in time.

"Where is she?" Cutter snapped.

"I don't know."

"You bastard."

"Come on, Sean…"

"I've got to go."

"Let her do this. I know you don't want to put her at risk, but we need her."

Cutter disconnected before the other man could say more. Without pausing, he dialed his old cell phone number, praying she would answer.

"Cutter?"

The sound of her voice shook him so thoroughly that for a moment he couldn't speak. When he finally found his voice, it was thick with emotion. "I've been trying to call you."

"I couldn't pick up."

"Why not? Are you—"

"Because I didn't know what to say."

He sighed. "Are you okay?"

"I'm fine."

"Where are you?"

She hesitated. "I'm in a safe place."

He gripped the phone tighter. "Mattie, tell me where you are."

"I can't."

"Damn it, don't do this."

"Evidently you've talked to Wolfe."

"He filled me in on your little scheme. If I didn't know better I'd think you have a death wish."

"Quite the contrary, Cutter. My only wish is to get my life back."

"Not like this."

"It's the only way."

"Mattie, damn it, where are you?"

Another hesitation. Longer this time. Damn, he was losing her. "Tell me where you are. I'll meet you. We'll talk about this."

"No. I know you'll try to stop me. I just wanted to let you know I'm okay."

"You're not okay!" he shouted.

"I have to go. I'll call you."

"Don't hang up."

"I'm sorry," she whispered.

Panic gripped him at the finality in her voice. "Mattie, you have to trust me on this. Damn it, I care about you."

But the line went dead.

Chapter Fifteen

Hanging up the phone was one of the most difficult things Mattie had ever had to do. She hated doing that to him. She'd felt the tension coming through the line. She'd heard the concern in his voice. She believed him when he said he cared about her.

But that was exactly why she couldn't do as he asked.

Dropping the phone into her pocket, she rose on shaking legs and looked through the window at the wire office across the street. The clerk at the desk had told her it would take an hour for the wire to go through. She checked her watch.

Only forty-five minutes had passed. She watched a group of people on the sidewalk in front of the office and wondered if The Jaguar or his thugs were already waiting for her to show up....

With fifteen minutes to kill, Mattie went to the counter and ordered another coffee. Taking a seat at one of the bistro tables near the front window, she watched the wire office. She checked her watch again. She drank the coffee, her nerves grinding. Finally it was time to call Cutter.

Dread gripped her as she punched in the numbers to his cell phone. "Cutter, it's me."

"Mattie, where the hell are you?" Stress roughened his voice. She hated knowing she'd put it there. All she could do was pray things went the way she'd planned.

"Take it easy," she said. "I'm okay."

"Don't tell me to take it easy," he snapped. "Damn it, I'm worried about you."

Mattie wondered if he would ever

know how badly she'd needed to hear those words at that moment. "I'll be at the wire office on the edge of town in five minutes. There's a very high probability that The Jaguar or one of his thugs will be there looking for me."

"Don't do it."

"I need you there, Cutter."

"This is a bad idea."

"It's the only way I can get my life back."

"You can't get your life back when you're dead. Damn it, you're not armed. We don't have backup. For God's sake I don't know if I can make it there in five minutes!"

"I'm going to do this with or without you. Either you can help me, or you can walk away. Your choice."

A curse burned through the line. "Don't walk into the shop until you see me." The pitch of his voice changed, and Mattie knew he was moving, running. "I'm on my way. Wait for me."

Mattie looked at her watch. She knew

if Cutter arrived before she made contact he would stop her. As frightened as she was of facing The Jaguar alone, she couldn't let that happen.

"Five minutes." Disconnecting, she left the coffee shop and started for the wire office across the street.

Mattie's legs shook as she crossed the street. When she opened the door to the wire office the young clerk behind the counter looked up at her and smiled. "Hello," he said. "Can I help you?"

She forced a smile that felt tremulous on her lips. She couldn't shake the feeling that she was in over her head. Could she really pull this off? Sick with fear, she strode to the counter.

"Could you please tell me if you've received a wire for me?" she asked.

"Let me check." He walked to a computer and began punching keys. "Let's see. What's your name?"

"Donna Clark."

"Clark." He typed in her name. "Where's it coming from?"

"Washington, D.C."

Frowning, he tapped the pencil against the counter. "Oh, here we are. Looks like it just came through." He grinned at her. "You have good timing."

Mattie wasn't so sure and looked over her shoulder through the office's window. Beyond, on the sidewalk, a heavy-set woman and a toddler in a bright-red coat were walking by. A young man with long hair was exiting a lime-green Volkswagen. No sign of anyone suspicious. No sign of Cutter.

Until now it hadn't crossed her mind that The Jaguar wouldn't show. Maybe he'd realized this was a trap. A new layer of worry enveloped her as she turned back to the clerk. He was still working on her wire. She didn't care about the money. All she wanted was for The Jaguar to show up so Cutter could take him in. She wanted this nightmare to be over.

She'd only been there for a minute, but it felt like an eternity. Why hadn't The Jaguar shown up? Where was Cutter?

She turned back to the counter. The clerk was reaching for something beneath the cash register. Absently she glanced through a partially open door behind the counter that led to a rear office. The lights were off. But in the dim light slanting through the door, she saw two feet sticking up, as if someone were lying on the floor. What on earth?

Her gaze snapped to the clerk. But his eyes were already on hers. And she suddenly knew he wasn't some inept clerk at all.

"Hello, Mattie," he said.

Terror whipped through her. For a moment she was paralyzed with it. Then she scrambled back and spun toward the front door, her only thought to get out and run for her life.

But she wasn't fast enough.

Midway there something stung her

shoulder. Heat raced up her arm. At first she thought she'd been shot. Then she looked down at her shoulder and saw a tiny dart protruding. A thousand terrible thoughts rushed through her mind. *Oh, dear God,* she thought, *help me.*

The drug slammed into her brain with the force of a sledgehammer. One moment she was running toward the door. The next she was lying on the floor on her belly, totally paralyzed, her mind reeling.

Why couldn't she move?

She saw the man vaulting the counter and walking over to her. She saw his boots, khaki slacks. He knelt and peered into her eyes. "Don't worry," he said. "The drug won't hurt you."

"Let me go," she slurred.

Smiling, he snapped his fingers. Two more men entered the room. "Take her to the van. Quickly."

"Yes, sir."

She tried to fight the arms that lifted her, but her muscles refused to cooperate.

They carried her to the rear of the store and to a waiting SUV in the alley.

"Cutter," she whispered as they opened the side door and shoved her inside.

The man looked down at her, an evil grin on his face. "Not even Sean Cutter can help you now," he said and slammed the door.

CUTTER SENSED DANGER the moment he burst into the wire shop. "Mattie!" he shouted.

The silence mocked him.

Darting across the customer waiting area, he slapped both hands down on the counter, his eyes scanning the clerk's work area where a single door stood ajar. "Hello! Is anyone here?"

He didn't wait for a response. Jumping over the counter, he drew his weapon and went toward the door. He kicked it open the rest of the way, scanned the murky interior, then leaned in and flipped on the light.

The clerk's body had been tucked

against the wall. The young man lay facedown in a pool of blood. Even before checking the clerk's carotid artery, Cutter knew he was dead.

You screwed up, a little voice accused.

Cutter was no stranger to the dark emotions that came with his line of work. But the knowledge that a man like The Jaguar had Mattie made his blood run cold.

It was his worst nightmare. He'd always believed that enduring torture was the worst thing he would ever face. But he'd been wrong. It was infinitely worse knowing the woman he loved was going to face the same horrors.

Cursing himself, he wished like hell he'd handled things differently.

He pulled the cell from his belt and hit Wolfe's number. The other man picked up on the first ring.

"The Jaguar has her." Cutter barely recognized his own voice.

"How long ago?" Wolfe asked.

"Less than five minutes."

"Let me scramble some agents." Papers rustled on the other end. "Are you at the wire office?"

"Yeah."

"Stay put."

"Damn it, Martin, you shouldn't have condoned this."

"She would have done it, anyway. Besides, I knew you were there."

"What you're really telling me is that she's expendable. If she can pull this off kudos to the CIA. If she doesn't, no big loss. Right, Martin?"

"If you weren't so emotionally involved in this you'd see it was the only thing I could have done."

"Yeah, and now I'm going to do the only thing I can."

"Sean, damn it, don't do anything stupid. We can still salvage this."

Cutter disconnected. The initial shock of terror was wearing off. His brain was beginning to function. He knew this was probably going to cost him his job, but he didn't think twice about calling in the only men he knew could help him save Mattie's life.

Mike Madrid answered with a gruff utterance of his name.

"I'm initiating a Code 99," Cutter said.

Madrid hesitated, then said, "What's the situation?"

Cutter rapidly summarized everything that had happened. "We've got to get to Logan before The Jaguar…" He couldn't finish the sentence. The mere thought of Mattie enduring the same horrors he had was simply too much to bear.

"Easy, Cutter," Madrid said. "We'll get her."

"For God's sake, Mike, he's going to torture her. We don't know the location of the compound."

The silence that followed was deafening.

"The Jaguar has a weak link," Cutter said. "But I need your help."

"Tell me and I'm there."

He told Madrid about Mattie's coworker, Daniel Savage. "I believe he's the one who framed her. There's a possibility he'll know the location of the compound. We know he's been in contact. If we can get his cell phone we can do a triangulation and find the nearest tower."

"Where's Savage?"

"D.C."

"I can be there in half an hour. I'll pay him a visit, see what I can get out of him."

"No holds barred."

"Roger that," Madrid said. "What's your twenty?"

"Silver Lake, Alberta."

"I'll scramble the Lear." Madrid paused. "It's still going to take a couple of hours."

"Let's hope Mattie can hang on that long."

"If I were you I'd start praying," Madrid said, and disconnected.

Chapter Sixteen

Mattie woke to the glare of a bright light. She was lying on her side with her knees pulled up protectively to her chest. She blinked, and a wall painted two-tone institutional beige came into view. She shifted, straightened and tested her limbs. Everything appeared to be in good working order. In the distance she could hear the clang of steel against steel.

At first she thought she had somehow landed in prison. Then she remembered walking into the wire office. The dead clerk. The man behind the counter. Sean Cutter just minutes away...

Gasping, she sat up and looked around.

She was in a small cell with a concrete floor and steel bars on one side. There were no windows, just a single light overhead, and she got the sensation of being underground.

Beyond the bars, a man wearing a brown paramilitary uniform sat with his boots propped on a scarred wooden desk, watching her with piggish eyes.

"Where am I?" she asked.

Never taking his eyes from hers, he reached for the phone and punched numbers into the keypad. "She's awake," he said and hung up.

Mattie shivered. Where on earth was she? What did The Jaguar have planned for her? She thought of how worried Cutter must be, and pain twisted inside her. He'd been right all along. He'd known she was in over her head. That she was unequipped to handle a brutal man like The Jaguar. And now here she was, in mortal danger.

"Ah, Ms. Logan, you're awake."

She rose abruptly at the sound of the deep, cultured voice. A chill swept through her when she found herself staring at The Jaguar. He was shorter than she'd imagined. Well under six feet. But what he lacked in physical stature he made up for with the power of his presence. He was an attractive man with eyes the color of bitter chocolate and the high cheekbones of a male model. His skin was flawless and olive. His hair glossy black and pulled into a neat ponytail at his nape.

Two men in uniform flanked him. Mattie stared at the pistols strapped to their hips, and the grave reality of the situation slammed home.

"Who are you and what do you want?" she asked.

"I think you already know the answer to both of those questions."

He reached the door to her cell and studied her for a moment. "I am The Jaguar," he said simply. "And you have something I want."

A shudder moved through her at the way he was looking at her. It was as if he was searching for the best place to hurt her.

One of the uniformed men removed a ring of keys from his belt and unlocked her cell door. The second man took out a set of nylon restraints from his belt.

"The real question," The Jaguar began, "is whether or not you're going to cooperate with me."

The two men entered the cell. Fear swept through her. *Oh dear God they're going to torture me,* she thought.

"I don't know what you're talking about," she heard herself say.

"Come now," The Jaguar said amicably. "Don't be coy. I know all about the EDNA Project." He smiled. "Well, almost everything, anyway. I'm particularly interested in phase two."

Only when the wall collided with her back did Mattie realize she had been backing up. The men converged on her.

There was no way she was going to be able to get away.

"Don't get any closer." She tried to sound authoritative, but her voice was high and tight with fear.

"They're not going to hurt you," The Jaguar said.

"I don't believe you." She stared at the cuffs, feeling trapped and more terrified than she'd ever been in her life.

A hint of a smile touched his mouth. "We're going to take you on a tour of the compound."

"I don't want a tour. I want you to let me go."

"I'm afraid I can't do that." He jerked his head at the man with the restraints. "Cuff her." His gaze swept to Mattie. "Don't fight them, Ms. Logan. You will not win."

She jolted when strong fingers wrapped around her arm and spun her around. Knowing there was no escape, she allowed the man to cuff her hands behind her back.

When she turned back to The Jaguar,

the smile had been replaced by a cruel light in his eyes. She saw that he was drawing a twisted sense of enjoyment from her fear.

"Shall we begin the tour?" Taking her arm, he motioned toward the steel reinforced door. "I believe once you've seen the facilities, you'll be ready to tell me everything you know about EDNA. An absolutely pain-free process I'm sure you'll appreciate."

As he guided her toward the door Mattie realized that just as Cutter had warned her, her fate was in the hands of a sociopath.

MIKE MADRID located Daniel Savage's condo and parked down the block. He entered the small backyard through the alley, using the hedge as cover from the prying eyes of neighbors. The security system was good, but Madrid was better. He chose the smallest point of entry—the downstairs bathroom window. He snipped wires to disable the sensor. In seconds he had the glass taped. Using the glasscutters, he scored the glass, tapped it out and removed it. A flick of his wrist and the lock snicked open.

He was in.

The condo smelled of eucalyptus oil and heated air. Soundlessly he left the bathroom and went into the darkened living room. Stairs to his left led to the second floor. The foyer and front door were straight ahead. The bedroom and study to his right. According to Savage's secretary, he was working from home today.

The first level of the condo was clear. With the silence and grace of a predatory cat, Madrid took the steps two at a time to the second floor. He paused on the landing and listened. There was a radio playing nearby, probably in the master bedroom. No sign of Savage.

His boots were silent against the carpet as he made his way to the bedroom. The door stood slightly ajar. He opened it the rest of the way. There were two forms huddled beneath a white down comforter. Removing the syringe from the compartment in his belt, Madrid walked to the bed and jammed the needle into the female's hip.

Yelling, she thrashed and turned over. Her eyes widened when she saw him. Then the fast-acting tranquilizer hit her system and she collapsed back into her pillow.

The commotion had wakened Daniel Savage. "What the—"

Madrid quickly subdued him. Cutter's words echoed in his ears as he slid the knife from its sheath and set it against Savage's carotid artery. "I'm going to ask you some questions," he said. "Every time you give me the wrong answer, I'm going to cut you."

"I…I have money. Take it. Please, don't hurt me."

"Shut up and listen," Madrid ordered.

"I need to know where The Jaguar's headquarters is located."

Confusion swam in Savage's eyes. "The Jaguar?"

Madrid made good on his word and cut him. Blood trickled onto the sheets. He shifted the crisp white cotton and made certain Savage could see his own blood. "Wrong answer."

Savage whimpered. "Please, don't…"

"Where is the compound? This time I won't miss the artery."

Daniel Savage began to talk.

CUTTER PACED the room for the hundredth time, he tried to get a grip on the fear spiraling inside him. He knew better than to operate on emotion. It was the fastest way to get someone killed. But he'd never felt so helpless in his life. It tore him up to think of Mattie, of the horrors she might be enduring.

Cutter still remembered with stark and frightening clarity every second of agony

The Jaguar had inflicted. He remembered the odd light of excitement in the other man's eyes, and he'd realized The Jaguar was so good at what he did because he enjoyed it.

For a moment Cutter thought he would be sick. Dear God how had the situation spiraled so horribly out of his control?

Hold on, Mattie, he thought. *I'm coming for you.*

The problem was he had no idea where to look for her. He'd searched the scene thoroughly, but The Jaguar had not left a single clue. Cutter had gotten on the phone and called in favors, but not even his shadier connections knew where The Jaguar's mountain compound was located.

The only information the MIDNIGHT Agency intelligence people could come up with was that the place was a fortress set on a hundred acres of rugged mountain terrain somewhere in Alberta, an immense province in western Canada. A lot of ground to cover. Without GPS coordinates, searching for her would be futile.

"Damn it!" Cutter slammed his fist down on the tabletop. "Madrid, where the hell are you?"

He glanced at his watch. Almost two hours had passed, and he knew all too well how much could have happened to Mattie by now. Cutter had never been good at waiting, but he honestly felt as if he were about to unravel.

He jolted when his cell phone chirped. Madrid's cell number appeared on the display. "Talk to me," he said.

"I got the GPS coordinates." Madrid rattled off a series of numbers. "I'm en route in the Lear. Backup is on the way. We'll meet you at the compound in three hours. Your instructions are to not go in alone."

Cutter made a bitter sound that was part growl, part laugh. "In three hours he'll have the plans for EDNA and Mattie will be dead."

"Sean, you need to calm down and think about this."

"Don't tell me to calm down, damn it."

"Look, Wolfe briefed me on the situation. Our objective is to take down The Jaguar. We can't afford to screw this up, Cutter. Come on. Work with me. There are a lot of lives at stake."

Cutter started for the door. "There's only one life I'm interested in at the moment."

"I don't want her getting hurt any more than you do, but you have to weigh her life against the lives of tens of thousands at risk if that bastard gets his hands on EDNA."

"I know what's at stake," Cutter snapped.

"The scientist is expendable, Sean."

"Yeah, well, so am I."

After ending the call, Cutter left the bed and breakfast at a dead run.

THE JAGUAR GAVE HER the grand tour of the compound as if he were the host of some upscale resort. Had it not been for the knot of fear tightening around her throat, Mattie could almost have imagined she was visiting the mansion of some celebrity in Los Angeles or New York or Chicago. But the reality that she was a prisoner in the lair of a killer never left her mind.

The dining rooms were massive and furnished with expensive Italian furniture. The chef's kitchen gleamed with stainless steel appliances and ornate tiles set into the walls. Antique furniture adorned the six guest bedrooms.

The Jaguar himself was nothing like she envisioned. He was cultured and soft-spoken. But as he went on about the compound and his reasons for having built it, Mattie saw something dark in his eyes. A deepseated hatred for anyone who did not agree with him. A total disregard for human life. A cruelty that was beyond frightening.

"Are you ready to begin the second phase of the tour?"

The question drew her from her reverie.

Mattie looked at him to find his eyes already on her, calculating, probing. She suppressed a shudder. "I want you to let me go," she said.

"Come now," he cooed. "You know I can't do that."

"You can. Please. I don't know anything about what you want."

Amusement danced in his eyes. "That remains to be seen, doesn't it?"

He wants to hurt me almost as badly as he wants the future plans for EDNA, she thought, shivering with terror.

The Jaguar nodded at one of the two men with them. The man punched numbers into a keypad set into the wall. A heavy door slid open to a murkily lit stairwell. The Jaguar motioned her inside. "Please," he said.

When Mattie hesitated, one of the other men gave her a shove. Knowing she didn't have a choice, she went down the stairs. At the base of the stairs, they entered a narrow hall with two doors on either side.

The steel doors were equipped with barred windows.

A scream shattered the silence. The sound was so shrill and animalistic, she couldn't tell if it was male or female. Then a second scream rent the air. The urge to put her hands over her ears to block out the horrific sound was overwhelming, but her hands were secured behind her back.

"In case you're wondering, this is the interrogation wing." The Jaguar motioned down the hall. "Shall we?"

"I don't want to see any more," Mattie said.

"All of my interrogation equipment is state-of-the-art." He went on as if he hadn't heard her. "Much of it was imported from other countries. Some of it I invented myself. You see, I am a master of persuasion. I know how to make people *cooperate*."

Taking her arm, he forced her down the hall, stopping at the first door. "This room is for level-one interrogations. I would take you inside, but as you can see it is currently in use. Observe," he ordered.

The last thing she wanted to do was look through the small window. She had no desire to witness the horrors going on inside any of these rooms. Lowering her head, Mattie shut her eyes. The next thing she knew strong hands were clamped around her head, forcing her face to the glass.

"Look at him!" The Jaguar commanded.

Mattie opened her eyes. She caught a glimpse of bare flesh. The stark red of blood. The jangle of chains against concrete. The crack of electricity against wet skin. A cry of anguish escaped her at the sight of the man's face as it contorted in agony....

"You're a monster," she whispered.

"I am a man fighting for what I believe is right."

"Not like this."

"How then?" Stepping in front of her he put his hand beneath her chin and forced her gaze to his. "Negotiation? Peace treaties?" His laugh was bitter. "Too many of my people have died trying."

"What do you want from me?"

She immediately regretted the question. She knew what he wanted. And she had a terrible feeling she knew how far he would go to extract it.

"I want the future plans for EDNA," he said. "You tell me what you know, and I'll let you go. I won't hurt you. I'll personally drive you to the nearest city and release you. It's as simple as that."

The offer was tempting. But Mattie knew that to accept it she would be making a deal with the devil. She knew that by relaying the information, tens of thousands of lives would be in danger. She'd never be able to live with herself even if he kept his word and let her live, which was highly doubtful.

"I don't know the future plans for EDNA," she said.

"Lying to me now will only cause you more pain later," he said.

"I swear," she said. "I don't know anything."

He stared at her with those cold, dark eyes. "Daniel Savage gave me your notes. You had outlined the second phase of EDNA. I know you were working on miniaturization. I know you had almost perfected it. I want those plans, Mattie, and I want them now. If you do not cooperate, I will be forced to take you into that room."

At that moment she was more terrified than she'd ever been in her life. She knew if she wanted to survive this she was going to have to talk. But the idea of unleashing any part of the EDNA project on an unsuspecting population repulsed her so thoroughly, she couldn't bring herself to say the words. There was simply no way she could give that kind of power to a terrorist.

Maybe she could make something up.

She could recreate her research and embellish it in a way that would ensure the weapon he built wouldn't work. She could design phony blueprints using substandard materials. After all, no one would be the wiser until the weapon was built and tested....

The level-one interrogation room door swung open. Mattie saw two men drag out a third wearing nothing more than a pair of drawstring pants. Her stomach turned when she noticed that his feet were leaving a trail of blood on the concrete floor.

"Ah, they've finished." The Jaguar smiled. "Take her inside."

She lunged backward in an attempt to free herself, but the two men snagged her arms.

"No!" she screamed as they forced her into the room. *"No!"*

The room was small, perhaps twelve feet square. A gurney sat against the wall. Chains with shackles hung from the ceiling. Electrical probes dangled from a table. An array of sharp instruments lined the counter.

Mattie looked down, saw a pool of blood the size of a saucer on the floor and tried not to imagine the horrors that had just taken place in this terrible room.

"What do you think of my interrogation room?" The Jaguar asked.

"I think you're a sick bastard," she said.

One side of his mouth curved. "I'm going to enjoy teaching you some manners."

"Go to hell!" she hissed.

"You first." He nodded at the two men. "Strap her to the gurney. Let her get a sense of who's in charge and who is not."

Mattie frantically looked around, but there was nowhere to run. No way to escape what this man had planned for her. She backed away as the two men approached her. With her wrists bound, there was nothing she could do to protect herself. The scars on Cutter's body flashed in her mind's eye. Only now did she realize fully the horrors he must have endured.

As the men dragged toward the gurney, Mattie felt as if she was entering hell.

Chapter Seventeen

Cutter stole the SUV at gunpoint just two blocks from the wire office. A man, probably on his way to the ski slopes, judging from his clothes and the snow chains on the tires, was sitting behind the wheel at a stoplight, tapping his fingers to the beat of a song on the radio. Cutter walked up to the passenger door and jammed the pistol into the side of his face.

"I'm a federal agent," he said. "This is an emergency. I'm commandeering your vehicle. Put your hands up and get out."

The man's eyes widened, his hand reaching for the knob. "Wh—whatever you say," he said.

"Get out. *Now.*"

The man slid from the seat and stumbled from the vehicle. Cutter hit the gas and left him standing in the street. By the time he reached the edge of town, he was doing sixty miles per hour, driving like a madman through deep snow and icy patches. The vehicle slid dangerously close to the ditch several times, but Cutter didn't slow down.

He'd located a sporting goods store while waiting for Madrid to call with the coordinates. There, he'd bought tools: wire cutters, flashlight, hunting knife, even a cheap GPS unit. He'd plugged in the coordinates and mapped out a route to the compound. It would be tough going, but if he could keep up this pace he could be there in half an hour.

"Hang on, Mattie," he whispered as he maneuvered a curve at a treacherous speed.

The passage of time hammered at him as the vehicle sped into the darkness and snow. Fear chased him no matter how fast he drove. Cutter had endured some of the worst things a human being could face. But the thought of Mattie facing the same fate at the hands of The Jaguar tore down his defenses like nothing else ever had in his life.

He made the half-hour drive in twenty minutes. He checked the GPS coordinates twice, fearing he had somehow missed the place. He took the SUV down a narrow stretch of dirt road when suddenly through the thick trees he saw the lights of the compound.

Nestled between two ridges, the place, built into the side of a mountain, was fortresslike. It was protected from the air by the high cliffs, protected from access by land because the roads were narrow and dirt. The perfect location for a terrorist training center.

He cut the headlights and eased the four-wheel drive vehicle down the narrow road. Even with the chains, the tires spun in the deep snow. At the half-mile point, fearing the vehicle would be seen, Cutter ran the truck into a deep ravine and set out on foot. He ran quickly in the darkness, knowing he had to reach Mattie before The Jaguar began his terrible work.

The compound was a massive stone-and-brick structure. Concertina wire surrounded the outer perimeter. Though he couldn't see them because of the falling snow, Cutter knew there would be spotlights, motion detectors and, of course, armed sentries. The Jaguar hadn't become the most powerful terrorist in the world by being lax in his security.

No, he would have it all and then some.

He approached the building from the north, used the wire cutters to make an opening in the concertina wire and crawled through on his belly. Once through the wire, Cutter jumped to his feet and looked around. He was twenty yards from the main building. From where he stood, he could see a guard tower. Dual spotlights shone from each corner of the building and swept the grounds in ten-second intervals.

Using the snow for cover, he sprinted to the north wall and flattened himself against the brick. No doubt all the entrances would be locked down tight. The windows were high and more than likely rigged to an alarm system.

The sound of a door opening startled him. Twenty feet away a man in a blue parka stepped outside. Cutter pressed closer to the brick and watched as the man pulled out a pack of cigarettes, tapped one out and lit up.

I just found a breach in your security system, you son of a bitch.

He waited until the man had finished smoking and punched the reentry numbers into a keypad. The second the door opened, Cutter took him out with a single blow from the wire cutters. He confiscated the man's assault rifle and uniform, then dragged him to a nearby stack of pallets where he would be out of sight. He gagged and bound him, then quickly changed into the uniform.

Cutter could feel the seconds ticking by as he entered the building. He couldn't stop thinking about Mattie. How frightened and alone she must feel. At that moment he would have given his own life to save hers. But he had to find her first.

Hang on, his mind chanted. *I'm coming for you.*

He slithered down a darkened tiled hall that intersected with another, wider hallway. In the distance he could hear heavy footsteps. The occasional slam of a steel door. Even in the dead of night the place was alive with evil.

Ever aware of the passage of time, Cutter headed toward the main part of the building. He was midway down the hall when a scream tore through the air.

The sound stopped him dead in his tracks. It was a sound so filled with terror that Cutter felt that same terror ripping through his own body.

Oh dear God, The Jaguar was torturing her.

Cutter closed his eyes against the images prying at his brain. He could not let himself think of her in personal terms because he knew it would render him useless. He leaned against the wall, struggled to overcome the dark emotions building inside him. But the fear and rage were so powerful that for a moment he could do nothing but stand there and shake.

Then he heard a second heartrending scream, and tried to discern where the scream had come from. To his right a steel door stood ajar. Cutter walked to the door and found himself looking down a steep and dimly lit stairwell.

Beyond, he heard voices. Heavy footfalls against concrete. The clang of steel against steel. He'd found The Jaguar's inner sanctum.

Forgetting caution, Cutter stepped into the darkness and started into a place he could only describe as hell on earth.

MATTIE HAD THOUGHT she had been mentally prepared for what she knew would happen. But as the men strapped her to the gurney, she knew no human mind could ever prepare for the horrors of torture.

She lay on the cold, hard gurney and listened to The Jaguar gather the tools of his trade. She struggled against the straps binding her, but the nylon restraints remained secure. Panic assailed her. But there was no escape. No hope. The best she could wish for was a quick end.

She'd vowed not to cry, not to beg. But the realization that her life was going to end at the hands of an evil man like The Jaguar sent a sob to her throat. So many things left undone. So many words left unsaid. She would never marry. Never bear children.

She would never have the chance to tell Cutter she'd fallen in love with him.

To find love now and never have the opportunity to say the words was bittersweet. The irony of it broke her heart.

"I believe we are ready to begin."

Every nerve in her body drew taut at the sound of The Jaguar's voice. Mattie raised her head. He stood facing her a few feet away, a tray in his hands.

"There's still time to do this the easy way." Crossing to her, he set his hand against her cheek. "It really would be a shame to mess up that pretty face." His fingertips slid down her throat, pausing at the valley between her breasts. "You are so very lovely."

Repulsed, Mattie shuddered.

"I was married once, you know. Her name was Monique, and she was every bit as beautiful as you are. Has Cutter told you about her yet?"

Mattie didn't know what to say. Cutter had told her about Monique, but acknowledging that would likely only fuel his sadism, so she said nothing.

"No matter." He waved the question away. "I loved her very much. I had to kill her, you know. You see, she slept with Sean Cutter and I do not share my women with anyone."

Mattie could hear her labored breaths echoing within the confines of the small room. She couldn't stop trembling.

Cutter, where are you?

"I want you to tell me about the next phase of the EDNA Project."

"What do you want to know?"

"Playing dumb does not become you," he said nastily. "It certainly will not buy you time." To prove his point he touched her leg with an electrical probe.

The spark of electricity sounded like a gunshot. The pain wrenched a scream from her throat. Her body jolted violently. Her vision swam. Sweat beaded her forehead even though the room was chilly. Oh dear God, don't let him do this…

"Just a little test," he said. "You see, I can give pleasure or I can inflict pain. The choice is yours."

"Tell me what you want to know," Mattie said in a quivering voice.

"I want to know about the next phase, of course," he said, picking up the probe again.

Mattie choked back tears. She knew even if she told him what he wanted to know he would not let her go. He would not let her live. The only thing she could do now was try to come up with a convincing lie so this wretched excuse for a human being could not use the technology she had invented against the free world.

"I-in the f-final phase of EDNA," she began, "we were going to begin work on miniaturization."

"Excellent. You're an extremely intelligent woman, Ms. Logan." The Jaguar put down the probe. "You see how it works? You speak to me, and the pain stops. Sean Cutter never got that."

Hot tears burned her eyes, but she blinked them back. She wondered where Cutter was. If he was frantic with worry and trying to find her at this very moment? *I'm sorry…*

"Untie me," she tried.

A cruel smile twisted his mouth. "I will release you after you tell me what I want to know."

"Or maybe you're a lying son of a bitch and plan to kill me even after I tell you what you want to know."

Something utterly terrifying flickered in the depth of his eyes. "I am a man of my word." He opened a drawer, pulled out a tiny hand recorder and turned it on. "Now, tell me about the miniaturization phase of EDNA or I will have no recourse but to hurt you. Next time I will not stop when you scream."

Lying there bound and helpless and trembling uncontrollably, she began to speak. In a shaking voice she told him about an early phase of EDNA. Unbeknownst to The Jaguar, it was a phase that had later failed during the testing stage. The theory had been good, but when the system was tested, fatal flaws were discovered.

The Jaguar recorded her every word. All the while she prayed Daniel Savage hadn't already spoken about the failed program. She knew The Jaguar would eventually see through the lies. But if she was lucky, lying to him now might buy her some time.

Hope came to a grinding halt when the door swung open. Mattie's gaze flew to the door. A chill passed through her when a man in paramilitary fatigues stepped into the room.

"I just spoke to Savage." He thrust an accusing finger at Mattie. "She's lying."

The Jaguar turned to her, his eyes glittering with anger and sadistic anticipation. "Ah, Ms. Logan, you disappoint me."

"I'm not lying," she choked.

"You should have known I would discover such an unsophisticated ploy." He picked up the probe and frowned. "You've left me no choice but to do this the hard way," he said and started toward her.

CUTTER TOOK OUT the sentry with the knife. He dragged the body into a utility closet and locked the door. The screams had stopped, but they'd rattled him badly. Deep in the bowels of The Jaguar's compound, he realized the place was much more than the nerve center for a terrorist cell. There were elaborate laboratories where, he suspected, scientists from all over the world converged to create weapons of mass destruction. There were underground gun ranges. But the worst thing Cutter saw were the torture chambers. He could smell the terror. A smell that conjured up memories he could not let himself dwell on.

He approached a T where another hall intersected. At the sound of voices, he stopped and peered around the corner. Two men with automatic rifles stood just outside a steel door, smoking cigarettes. One of the men he recognized as The Jaguar's personal bodyguard. A man who never left The Jaguar's side. And Cutter knew he'd found Mattie.

Breathing hard, he pressed his back against the wall. He darted past the hall and kept going. There was no way he alone could take out two men with automatic weapons. There was no cover. Even if he was lucky enough to take out the two men, the commotion would alert The Jaguar and allow him time to harm Mattie....

Feeling desperate, Cutter kept walking. He went through a double set of steel doors and entered a separate wing. He glanced through the tiny window of a steel door as he passed by it. Within he saw bars and concrete—and stopped dead in his tracks. Prisoners. Looking both ways, he ducked through the door. The single guard looked up from his desk when Cutter approached.

"What the—"

Cutter slammed the wire cutters against the man's temple. Using the last of his rope, he bound the man's hands and feet. He fished the ring of keys from the guard's pocket, then stood and faced the cells.

A dozen or more men looked out at him. Their eyes were sunken and flat. Many were injured. All looked half-starved. "I'm an American," Cutter said. "I'm freeing you. Help will be here any minute now. Do you understand?"

One of the men stepped forward. Reaching out, he dropped to his knees. "Thank God," he said with a German accent.

"Who are you?" Cutter asked.

"I am a scientist from the university in Frankfurt," the man replied. "I was kidnapped by terrorists two months ago."

"Ransom?" Cutter asked.

"They're forcing me to help them build a weapon of mass destruction," the man said with disgust.

"Are there any more prisoners besides all of you?"

The man shook his head. "This is all that's left."

Cutter went to work unlocking the cells. "I'm here to rescue a young woman," he said to the men. "A scientist. She's in grave danger. I need your help to save her life."

The men left their cells and shuffled closer. "You just saved our lives, mate," a man with an Australian accent said. "Tell us what to do and we'll do it."

Cutter picked up the guard's rifle and handed it to the Australian. Their eyes met, and a silent understanding passed between the two men.

"I need a diversion," Cutter said.

A murmur of enthusiasm went through the men. He figured most were scientists or researchers or engineers. Family men whose scientific knowledge or job had put them in danger. Even though they were from different countries with different beliefs and religions—and weakened from weeks of starvation and torture—not one of them refused.

Leaning close, Cutter lowered his voice. "Here's what I want you to do."

Chapter Eighteen

Mattie struggled against the binds, but her efforts were in vain. But even facing death and the fear that in the end she would probably talk, her thoughts were on Cutter. On the future they would never have. The sense of loss devastated her.

"Rest assured, Ms. Logan, you *will* tell me what I want to know."

The Jaguar set a tray of instruments on the table next to her. Her heart pumped out of control in her chest at the sight of the syringe.

"Pain serum," he said. "A simple subcutaneous injection and my work is... well, no more than mere observation. I developed it last year after a particularly difficult subject. It attacks the nerves with no or little damage to the surrounding tissue. Therefore, a subject's, shall we say, endurance is much enhanced."

He picked up a second vial filled with a liquid the color of weak coffee. "This is the antidote. One injection and the pain disappears." He snapped his fingers. "Like magic."

"You're a pathetic excuse for a human being," Mattie said.

"No," he replied. "I simply enjoy my work." He nodded at the other man in the room. "Leave me to my work."

"Yes, sir." The man nodded brusquely and left the room.

The Jaguar filled the syringe. One filled with hell. The other with salvation. Tears scalded her cheeks. *Oh, Cutter, I'm sorry I got us into this nightmare....*

Once both syringes were prepared, The Jaguar turned to her and brandished the pain serum filled syringe like a jewel. "Are you ready, Ms. Logan?"

Mattie jumped when he leaned close and switched on the recorder. "Please," she said. "I don't know anything more about the program than what I've already told you."

The Jaguar assessed her. "Even if you're telling the truth, I want to make certain Sean Cutter hears your final screams."

Mattie felt ill at the thought of what that would do to him. She knew he would blame himself for her death. The guilt would eat him alive. He would want revenge. "You know he'll come for you."

"Ah, but I'm counting on it."

A hard rap on the door broke the moment. Mattie looked up to see one of The Jaguar's men stick his head in.

"I'm sorry to disturb you, but there's been a security breach in the prison," the man said.

The Jaguar snarled a curse. *Not because of the breach,* Mattie thought, *but because his work had been interrupted.* "What happened?"

"Six men have escaped. The guard tower is reporting shots fired at the north perimeter."

"Send all available men to round them up."

The man grimaced. "Sir, there's no way these men escaped on their own. We think they had help."

"I want those men, and whoever helped them. Alive. Check the security cameras. I want to know how this happened."

The man saluted and left as quickly as he'd entered. Mattie's heart was pounding. Had Cutter been the cause of the security breach? Had he come to save her? To stop this madness? Hope burst through her at the prospect.

"Ah, you're thinking about him, aren't you?" The Jaguar asked.

Mattie shook her head. "No."

"You love him, no?"

"He's an agent. I'm his prisoner. That's all."

"He must care for you very much to face me after what I did to him two years ago. I understand he's healing nicely."

"I wouldn't know."

The Jaguar picked up the syringe. "I hate to be the bearer of bad news, Ms. Logan, but he's not going to get here in time to save you."

Mattie screamed when the needle pricked her arm. The initial burst of pain exploded through her body like a grenade. She heard herself cry out. She felt her muscles go rigid, her body jerking against the restraints.

The door swung open and banged against the wall. Through the veil of pain she saw The Jaguar swing around, the syringe falling to the floor. Cutter burst into the room. Gun trained on The Jaguar, his eyes swept to hers. In the last days she'd been through some intense situations with Cutter, but she'd never seen such fury in his eyes.

"You son of a bitch." He chambered a bullet.

The Jaguar raised his hands. "I'm unarmed," he said.

"I don't care." Cutter said, his eyes going to Mattie. "Are you all right?"

"P-pain serum," she gasped. "Oh God, Cutter, it's bad. Help me."

Cutter's attention went back to The Jaguar. "Get facedown on the floor. Now. Before I take you out right here and now like the piece of scum you are."

The Jaguar glanced at Mattie. "I see you're very fond of her."

"Do it!"

A chilling smile whispered across The Jaguar's face. "She's a trooper, Cutter. But then, I'd barely begun. Unlike you, she would have talked. You're an anomaly, you know. My greatest failure. I'd always hoped to rectify my shortcomings with you. Perhaps one day we can—"

A gunshot shattered the silence. Mattie cried out, unsure at first from whence it had come. Then she realized Cutter had pulled off a shot to let The Jaguar know he was dead serious. *"Now,"* he said. "Or I'll put the next one between your eyes."

The Jaguar's eyes never left Cutter as he got down on the floor. The pain was so bad Mattie could barely breathe. It was as if every bone in her body had been broken. Even though Cutter had taken control of the situation, she couldn't shake the feeling that things were about to explode.

When The Jaguar was down on the floor, Cutter went to her. He touched her face with one hand as he worked the straps with the other. "What can I do?"

"Antidote." Groaning in pain, she lifted her hand to point. "There."

Cutter snatched the syringe. Expertly thumbing off the cap, he set the needle against her shoulder and injected the antidote.

The pain dulled almost instantly. Though still hurting, Mattie at least felt as if she could breathe. As if she could function. "Oh, God, Cutter, he was going to—"

"You're going to be okay, honey. Let me get these straps off you. Then I'll get you out of here, okay?"

"Hurry."

Setting the syringe on the counter, he withdrew a knife and cut the straps with a quick flick of his wrist. Once her hands were free, Mattie worked frantically to free herself. But her hands were shaking so badly she had a difficult time. Cutter took a length of one of the straps and turned to The Jaguar, who was still face-down on the floor.

"Put your hands behind your back," Cutter ordered.

The Jaguar complied. Mattie worked at the last strap on her leg. She'd been so close to suffering a terrible death. She owed Sean Cutter her life.

Out of the corner of her eye she saw Cutter holster his weapon so he could secure The Jaguar's wrists. *It's almost over,* she thought. They were going to get out of this alive. Her name would be cleared. The Jaguar would pay for his crime. The terrorist cell would be dismantled. Finally she and Cutter could be together....

Hope turned to horror when The Jaguar twisted. Cutter went for his weapon, but he wasn't fast enough. The Jaguar jabbed the syringe into the side of Cutter's neck.

"Cutter!"

Mattie knew it the moment the drug hit his brain. His body went rigid. His mouth pulled into a taut line. His hand shook as he brought up the gun.

The Jaguar jumped to his feet, lunged at Cutter. "Now we're going to finish this!"

Cutter scrambled back. The first shot went wide. There was no way he could shoot while in that kind of agony. She flung herself from the gurney. Her hand slammed down on the syringe of pain serum.

The Jaguar went for the gun in Cutter's hand. Cutter grabbed the other man's wrist and twisted, but the pain was taking a heavy toll. Wielding the syringe like a knife, Mattie raised it above her head and brought it down, jabbing it into The Jaguar's back.

Roaring, the man turned on her. "You *bitch!*" he screamed. "Look what you've done!"

Then the drug must have taken effect because she saw his body stiffen. His eyes widened. "Give me the antidote!" he cried. "Give it to me!" He reached for it, but before he could grasp it his knees buckled. An animalistic sound tore from his throat as he collapsed to the floor.

Mattie whirled to help Cutter. He lay sprawled on his back a few feet away, staring at the ceiling. His face was contorted in pain, his complexion the color of paste. Sweat beaded on his forehead. She knew firsthand how terrible the pain serum was, and a sick sense of helplessness assailed her.

He turned his head, and his eyes met hers. "Nice work," he ground out.

"Oh, Cutter." She dropped to her knees beside him.

"You okay?" he asked.

Mattie blinked back tears. Only Sean Cutter would ask that question while he was in the throes of a terrible agony. "I'm fine." She brushed her fingertips against his forehead. "You need the antidote."

"On the counter," he groaned, and closed his eyes.

Mattie jumped to her feet and looked around, spotted the syringe crushed on the floor. "Oh no," she whispered.

A few feet away, The Jaguar writhed in pain. Hatred burned in his eyes when he raised his head and looked at her. "You are a dead woman," he hissed.

Though the man was incapacitated with pain, a chill passed through her. She crossed to Cutter and knelt. "Cutter, I'm sorry. The syringe was crushed during the scuffle."

"Just my luck…"

"What can I do?"

"Why don't you just hang on to me for a second?"

Even through the pain, Mattie saw the light in his eyes. He was the most stoic human being she'd ever met.

"Touch me," he whispered. "It…helps."

Choking back tears, she settled onto the floor beside him and took his hand. "I'm sorry I left without saying anything."

"You nabbed a big fish. I'll yell at you later."

"It's a deal."

His face contorted, and Mattie's heart broke for him. "Cutter, I can't stand seeing you like this."

"Help…on the way. Should be here any… minute."

Relief swept through her with such force that for a moment she couldn't find her voice. "Your agency?"

"Men of MIDNIGHT. They're the best, you know."

"If they're half as good as you, we're in good hands." But a quiver of uneasiness went through her at the thought of being taken into custody.

"Don't worry," he whispered. "They know you're innocent. Just a...formality."

A sob escaped her at the realization that the nightmare was finally over. That she had her life back. That she was free to love this man. And suddenly she felt like the luckiest woman in the world.

Blinking back tears, she placed her hand against his face. "Thank you."

"Don't leave me again without saying goodbye."

"Wouldn't dream of it." Leaning close, she brushed a kiss against his forehead.

"Your kiss...better...than...antidote," he whispered.

"That's just the beginning," she whispered, and put her arms around him.

Chapter Nineteen

The room was so quiet Cutter could hear the heated air rushing through the vents. Martin Wolfe sat at the head of the table, looking down at the open manila folder in front of him. To his right, Mike Madrid leaned back in his chair, staring into the cup of coffee in his hands. Jake Vanderpol sat across from him, looking bored. Halfway down the table, a representative from the Department of Corrections and an assistant federal prosecutor huddled over paperwork.

Where was Mattie?

His mind had no more than formed the question when the door swung open. His heart stopped in his chest at the sight of her. She wore a fitted blue suit jacket and a skirt that fell conservatively to her knee. Her calves were slender and beautiful, and the sight of them reminded him of things he was definitely better off not remembering at a time like this. Her blond hair was swept into a roll at her nape. Her lipstick was the color of a cherry Popsicle. She wore tiny spectacles, but not even glasses could hide the magnificence of her eyes.

She looked nervous and so lovely it took a good bit of discipline not to go to her and throw his arms around her.

Martin Wolfe rose and extended his hand. "Mattie Logan, it's nice to finally meet you in person. I'm Martin Wolfe."

Her smile lit up the room as she accepted his hand. "Thank you for trusting me and letting me follow through with my plan."

"The MIDNIGHT Agency appreciates your courage and the sacrifice you made to help us apprehend The Jaguar."

"I had a vested interest."

"A grand jury will convene in your absence next week. At that point all charges will be officially expunged from your record. You will be compensated for any lost wages." Wolfe paused. "Today you will receive an official apology from the federal prosecutor's office and the Department of Corrections."

But her eyes were no longer on the agency head. Cutter felt it like a physical touch when her gaze landed on him. For a moment it was as if they were the only two people in the room. Memories swept through him. Their life-and-death struggle through the mountains. The first time he'd touched her. The first time he'd kissed her. The first time they'd made love.

"Cutter?"

He jolted at the sound of his name. He looked around, realized with some embarrassment that all eyes in the room were on him. He'd been staring at Mattie and didn't have a clue what had been said.

Four days had passed since their terrible ordeal at The Jaguar's compound in Alberta. Both Mattie and Cutter had been flown back to Chicago where they'd been thoroughly examined by the agency physicians and de-briefed. It had killed Cutter to see Mattie transported to a holding cell. Though all involved knew Daniel Savage had framed her and she was innocent, no one had had the authority to release her that first night.

Cutter hadn't slept for worrying about her.

"Your report?" Wolfe said.

Clearing his throat, Cutter rose. He hadn't prepared anything in writing. Most of his work was fieldwork; he wasn't very good at this sort of thing. But Mattie Logan wasn't the only one with a vested interest in this case. He had one, too. A big one.

"I just want to say that Mattie Logan was instrumental in the apprehension and arrest of the terrorist kingpin known only as The Jaguar." Cutter's gaze swept to the federal prosecutor. "This government at the very least owes her an apology."

His gaze locked with hers. "She put her life on the line multiple times. When I sustained a bullet wound, she administered first aid. She had many opportunities to escape. Instead she chose to risk her life to do the right thing. That included hatching a plan that ultimately led to the capture of a vicious terrorist. Without Mattie Logan's heroics I believe The Jaguar would still be a free man."

He stared at her, unable to look away. Tears filled her eyes, but she didn't make a sound. Even from fifteen feet away he could see that she was trembling. "I owe my life to her," he said. But his voice was little more than a whisper.

The room went silent. Before he realized he was going to move, he'd rounded the table. Mattie's eyes widened as he drew near. Upon reaching her, he took her hand and gently pulled her to her feet.

Then she was standing so close he

could discern the sweet scent of her perfume. He could feel the warmth emanating from her body to tantalize his. The sexual tension rising between them.

"I want you to know, I didn't plan on using you or putting you in danger. I sure as hell didn't plan on falling in love with you." Raising his hand, he thumbed a tear from her cheek. "But I did."

Tilting her head, Mattie pressed her face into his palm. She hadn't known what to expect of this formal meeting, but this was not it. "Cutter, I don't know what to say."

"Don't say anything," he answered, and pulled her into his arms.

"We've got an audience," she whispered.

"I don't care."

His heart pounded against hers. She reveled in the sensation of being in his arms.

Though Mattie was conscious of the other men rising and shuffling from the room, her attention remained focused on the man holding her in his arms

Martin Wolfe cleared his throat noisily.

Cutter pulled back and smiled down at her. Together they looked at the agency head.

Wolfe frowned, but Mattie saw the smile in his eyes. "This meeting is adjourned." He looked at Mattie. "A representative from the Department of Defense will be in contact with you. If you want your job back, it's yours for the taking. They can use all the talent they can get."

She hadn't yet decided how to handle getting her career back on track, but a phone call from her superiors was a good start. "Thank you."

"Now you two get out of here." Wolfe looked at Cutter. "You've got the next two weeks off. I suggest you make good use of it," he said, and left them alone in the conference room.

Grinning, Cutter looked into her eyes. "You're a free woman, Mattie."

"Where does this leave us?" she asked.

"Together."

"That's a good place to be."

"What do you say we check out the

beach somewhere in the Caribbean for the next week or so?" Leaning close he brushed a kiss to her mouth. "I hear the water's nice this time of year."

Mattie closed her eyes and held him close. "I thought you'd never ask," she said and kissed him back.

* * * * *

Look for Linda Castillo's next Harlequin Intrigue this September!

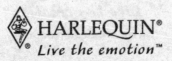

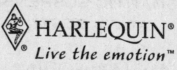

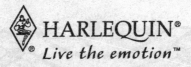

Harlequin Historicals®
Historical Romantic Adventure!

From rugged lawmen and valiant knights to defiant heiresses and spirited frontierswomen, Harlequin Historicals will capture your imagination with their dramatic scope, passion and adventure.

Harlequin Historicals . . . they're too good to miss!

HARLEQUIN®
Presents

The world's bestselling romance series...
The series that brings you your favorite authors,
month after month:

Helen Bianchin...Emma Darcy
Lynne Graham...Penny Jordan
Miranda Lee...Sandra Marton
Anne Mather...Carole Mortimer
Susan Napier...Michelle Reid

and many more uniquely talented authors!

Wealthy, powerful, gorgeous men...
Women who have feelings just like your own...
The stories you love, set in exotic, glamorous locations...

HARLEQUIN®
Presents

Seduction and Passion Guaranteed!

HPDIR104

eHARLEQUIN.com

The Ultimate Destination for Women's Fiction

Visit eHarlequin.com's Bookstore today
for today's most popular books at great prices.

- An extensive selection of romance books by top authors!

- Choose our convenient "bill me" option. No credit card required.

- New releases, Themed Collections and hard-to-find backlist.

- A sneak peek at upcoming books.

- Check out book excerpts, book summaries and Reader Recommendations from other members and post your own too.

- Find out what everybody's reading in Bestsellers.

- Save BIG with everyday discounts and exclusive online offers!

- Our Category Legend will help you select reading that's exactly right for you!

- Visit our Bargain Outlet often for huge savings and special offers!

- Sweepstakes offers. Enter for your chance to win special prizes, autographed books and more.

Your purchases are 100% guaranteed—so shop online at www.eHarlequin.com today!

INTBB104R